Dialogue Prompt

Chapter 1

It's the autumn of the year 2017 in Hampton Roads, Virginia. I'm a newspaper reporter working for the *Virginia Pilot Newspaper* based at our main office located in Norfolk, Virginia.

I've been working here as a reporter now for seven years. I started off in circulation and worked my way to something I've always wanted to do. Telling the truth about life in our community and abroad has always been a goal of mine. I read other newspapers from other states to remain informed, like the *New York Times, Chicago Tribune* and whatever paper has a newsworthy headline on the front page. I have a routine I practice every Thursday to randomly choose a newspaper from an area I rarely read about.

By the way, my name is Marc Dazet. I'm 32, married now for three years to a wonderful woman named Sundara Dazet and we have a daughter named Laura .
. . Alright, back to my original story. On Thursday, as I was explaining, I choose a newspaper of random choice to read their stories and watch the techniques of other reporters. Today I chose a paper from New Hampshire called *The Laconia Daily Sun*. We have a room at the office here where our reporters can choose newspapers to read to see what the competition is doing and to read about newsworthy events from all over the states.

So, today I picked a New Hampshire paper. Something catches my eye on the front page, bold lettering and headline:

**MAN FROM SEABROOK, NH WINS
THE POWERBALL LOTTERY FOR 429.6 MILLION**

I freeze and say to myself, "now this going to be a good story" and I start to drift for second as if I won the lottery myself. I start thinking what would I do with all of that "MONEY" for my family and friends. I'm still in pause mode as my reporter curiosity skills come back to reality to continue reading the story. It goes on to say he was the biggest winner in the state of New Hampshire and it looks like in the picture the whole town of Seabrook is there in the background of the photo. In the story, they ask what was he going to do with the money and he says he is planning on using the money to give future generations of his family a comfortable life. There was more to the story, but I just stopped reading and thought to myself, "Whoa I would like to meet this person for a story for our newspaper here in Virginia." I was thinking to myself, "Who does that." I folded the newspaper in my hands and walked out of the room.

As I was walking to my senior editor's office, I receive a text from my wife. "Hi honey, how's my newspaper man?" I text back, "I'm okay, your cookies you baked for me were good, had them with lunch." My wife replies, "You know I like baking for you Dazet". I told her "I have something to tell her later." She goes on and says "TELL ME NOW". "I can't now, but you know I will tell you when I get home". "Okay, you better tell me later or NO Cookies LOL". I put my Samsung 6 back in my holster and continue walking with the newspaper. As I was walking, my mind drifts back to the story in

NH and how I will tell our managing editor that I wanted to do a story on the winner. I paused, walking slower before getting to her office. I look up and on the wooden glass door I see the name 'Managing Editor Amelia Williams'. I knock on the door and I hear her voice say "Come in."

"Hi Amelia, how are you doing today and how the news world?"

"Well, it will be better when more solid news stories are reported," she responds.

"Well, here's what I was thinking. I'm due vacation time this fall and wanted to report on a story in New Hampshire."

She walks towards the window, looking at the traffic below to sigh and say, "Where in New Hampshire?"

I took off my glasses, laid them on the table so I could think of how to get her to okay this story. "A place called Seabrook."

 "Ummm what's the story about?" Then Marc puts back on his glasses excited to tell her what he wanted to report on.

Well, a man won the Lottery there."

Amelia pauses, pretending to show no interest in the story, turns around from the window and sits down in here chair, she goes on to say "Anddddd?"

Marc is now talking with his hands to his boss "Well, the story is not that he won, it's what he's going do with his winnings. He wants to give to the future generations of his family," I paused, clenching my hands. "I thought about that.This would be a good story. I thought I would ask first, you can think about it and call me if I can do the story."

Amelia stood up from her chair, put her hands to her chin in a thinking mode. I went into what they call a reporters panic mode, waiting for her answer. The five minutes it took her to think about it seemed like a ½ hour.

"Okay, I will call you in morning go home and wait for a call from me to see what to do next." I shook her hands and didn't say a word and walked out slowly from her office.

I started gathered my things from my desk, made a copy of the story from the Seabrook Newspaper. Walking straight to the parking garage, my thoughts were bouncing around about the story.

Took me some time to finally open the door of my Jeep Cherokee. I made a left turn on Brambleton Ave. Based in Norfolk VA. This area is divided into seven cities, I work in one city and live in another city called Virginia Beach. I have a condo on the ocean with my wife and daughter. It's a twenty-minute drive from work to home towards the oceanfront. I'm always amazed at the scenery of Hampton Roads, I have a nickname for people who live in this part of Virginia. I frequently say "The Water People". They're very unique, just like the characteristics of the ocean water . . . from dolphins to whales and swordfish, even sharks; this equals to the community where I live and work called Hampton Roads.

Arriving home I unlocked the door and I am greeted by my wife Sundara."Hi, honey, glad your home," she high fives me and bumps me with her elbow. While looking around our condo you can see both of our tastes in a mixture of items that personifies our personalities from fish nets with shells, antiques, and trendy furniture. There's a picture my wife brought of space; it looks like stars over an island under the caption it says "Andromeda Galaxy".

Our daughter Laura, is in her room doing homework. As I walk by her room she stands up with both hands in the air and waves while running to give me hug. "Hi, Dad how are you?"

"I'm doing fine honey. How was your day?"

Her hug stopped as she started looking around her room she pointed to her desk. "I'm fine, I was working on my homework and watching TV."

"Very good." She waited for the approval from me as her Dad. I put one finger in the air, as a jester of peace and that I would be back to talk with her more about her day. She knew instantly more talks about her day would happen later.

" I have to talk with your Mom, I'll be right back Laura, I promise." She smiled and pointed at me. I put down my laptop bag and took my shoes off, then proceeded to sit in my chair near Sundara. My wife smiles at me and the temperature of the room changes in a half of a second. I look at here and smile back.

 "It's good to be home, do you have any more of those cookies I had at work?" Then I saw her smile with humor. "Yes, I do but first you must tell

me what you wanted to say from work before you can have any more cookies."

Relaxing in my chair I get ready to tell my wife about the day, " Well you know today is Thursday?"

Sundara said, "Yes, it is and . . .?"

"Well, at the office I randomly choose a newspaper to read from another location in the States like every Thursday." As I was explaining the story I couldn't hide my excitement. "Well on the front page I read about a man who won the Lottery in a town called Seabrook, New Hampshire... Sundara becomes excited listening to the story to the point where she said my name twice.

"Marc, Marc. What's a Lottery?"

I forgot all of sudden who I was talking too. I told her we have a drawing in each state as I took a piece of paper to explain this better and tore it up in many pieces of paper which I put all in one in one container. I went on to explain our system raises money for charity and other local projects such as schooling, roads, etc... We buy tickets to win and I pointed to the container of papers shaped like a small mountain on the table.

Sundara looked at me with a strange with a smile. " How do you win?"

I can't believe I'm trying to explain the lottery to my wife. I told her 5 numbers are drawn from a group of 75 numbers and 1 number is drawn from

a number of 15. She tuned-in to listen more as I continued "and a player who buys the tickets must match all 6 numbers to win the jackpot prize we know as the lottery. I pointed to the papers again. "This pail papers on our table equals their winnings."

Sundara said, "I understand, now tell what happened today at the newspaper."

"Okay, well today as I was doing my Thursday routine of choosing a random paper in this small ocean town called Seabrook, New Hampshire on the front pages I read about a man who won the lottery."

My wife with excitement said, "he did" and she pointed to the pile of papers. And I said "yes".

It was almost like we won as I was explaining what happened to me at work.

"The thing that caught my eye was the man wants to share his winning money with future generations of his family so they can live comfortably. I want to find out more about this story and I thought that we have vacation time coming up so why don't we go to New Hampshire? We can go there, relax, and I can get an interview with him.

Sundara, in a pause mode, says "how about you go there for a few days alone and come back and we can spend the rest of our vacation camping near the lake."

"Umm, now that sounds like a plan…I have to wait for Amelia to okay the trip and the story. She said she would me call in the morning.

My wife looked at me for what seemed like five minutes and then asked how much did he win?

I pointed to the pail and said, "429.6 million." She leaped up from her chair and started cheering and clapping, Our daughter came in the living room wondering if anything was wrong ..I smiled at her and said, "everything was okay.

"Now can I have more cookies Sundara?"

"Yes there five left, save one for Laura, my husband.:

"I will try my best, don't want to rock the boat on the chocolate chip supply."
In the back of my mind, I am hoping Amelia calls in the morning with good news.

It's 9:30 am in the morning, I hear a ring on the nightstand for the third time and thought to myself "hopefully it's the call I was waiting for. I pick up the phone and Amelia says, " Hello Marc, how are you doing this morning?

I answered back half sleepy and half awake, "I will not know how my day is until I hear your answer about this story Amelia."

"That's fair to say, Marc," there was a pause on the phone and Marc thought the answer was going to be no, then Amelia's voice came over and said, "Okay Marc you have three days in New Hampshire to get the story. I will schedule an airline ticket and rental car for you at the Norfolk Airport to fly into the Seabrook, New Hampshire. See ya when you get back with a good story."

"Thank you, Amelia. Yes, I am having a good day so Far

"Bye, Marc."

"Bye, Managing Editor."

After the phone call was over, I stared at my phone in disbelief.

I hear my wife say, "Is everything okay?"

" Yes, everything is fine now. I can go on the trip to New Hampshire."

"Good."

I got up from bed to pack for my trip this afternoon.

Chapter 2

A couple hours later I hugged my wife and daughter and told them I will be back in a few days. I made sure I mentioned, we have more vacation days left together as a family.

I jump in my Jeep and start heading back to Norfolk to the airport. Flying out from the location was familiar because of the other stories I had a chance to be assigned to for the newspaper. I know the routine well. Each time there was a chance to fly, it's always a new the experience, except for the metal detector.

Taking off my shoes and putting my items in the plastic container and hearing the famous words… "Step Through Please". Glancing at the tickets, the flight time is not that bad, about an hour and 20 minutes landing at Portsmouth International Airport in New Hampshire. Seabrook was about a 12-mile drive from the airport. Time flies on a short trip.

As I'm landing, I notice two items right, away, that's different from Virginia, one the accents I hear called a 'New England accent'. No "R" in most of their speech and I know when they hear me speak they, will say I have the accent.

I didn't speak much, I was all ears listening to the accents of people walking about and taking it all in as I was learning the New England accent from New Hampshire. The second item I noticed was the weather compared to Virginia, a little bit colder. I walk over to the Hertz rental car area, gave them my information and they told me they have a car reserved for me right outside. I was wondering which car Amelia reserved for me. I like when she picks the rental cars, then I know not to go overboard with price choice and she is the boss.

She rented me a Full size 2017 Chevrolet Malibu. I'm happy with her choice, there's lots of room to move around. I called my wife to tell her that I have arrived safely in New Hampshire "Hi Honey, how are you doing? I'm here."

"I see", Sundara said. I can tell my wife was happy I made it in safely and sad I'm away from her and my daughter.

I spoke louder than normal in the airport concourse. " Did Laura get the extra cookies I left her"

In the background, I hear a voice yell out, "Yes, I got it" I smiled through the phone.

"Okay, just making sure, Honey I will keep you posted where I am.. please keep your Apple phone nearby," I told her I needed her here because of the weather its cold here. She laughed in Virginia.

As soon at the call ended. I mentally came back to New Hampshire. As if I came out of a phone booth like Clark Kent. I started my road trip to Seabrook from their airport in the car driving 55 miles per hour.

The scenery very nice. I couldn't even turn on the radio it was so nice to see during this time in the fall multi-color leaves on the ground and on trees, very outdoorsy feeling.

Great for the eyes and the fresh smell of fresh air…I'm understanding why many want to move here now…

It took me no time to arrive in the ocean town of Seabrook, there was a welcome sign reading **"Welcome to Seabrook Beach, New Hampshire"** I was staying at a hotel near the water called The Holiday Inn Express Hotel & Suites, it was at 11 Rocks Road. As I checked in I see the newspaper in the lobby *The Laconia Daily Sun* I read at the Pilot back home on the counter.

This time on the front page a news story about residents who will have the opportunity to become members of the state house of representatives. I didn't see hints or more stories about the lottery winner in the paper. It felt like the person who won vanished from community thoughts. I knew this wasn't true.

While in the hotel room relaxing, I thought, "let me reread the article to get more hints." I reach into my suitcase for the local paper and I thought to myself, I didn't catch the person's name here in New Hampshire, I look again focusing below the picture, I see the name, Brent Brooks. I write the name down in my notepad. I already had the other items for researching, on my smartphone and laptop.

I look around the room with all its amenities… the room seemed to hug you in comfort. While researching the winner of the lottery; I have pieces of paper everywhere. I work with a mad organizational purpose that only makes sense to me. This hotel room won't look the same when I check out.

I start to think it's time to Google his full name first. I put in the search bar "Brent Brooks, Seabrook, New Hampshire" and wait for the search engines feedback.

It said Coastal Beach Watershed, I wrote on my notepad, then I see American Motorcyclist, then another search read The Greenpeace Chronicles. I write all this all down. Then I thought, let me look at the picture again from the Lottery and I scan the picture like a hawk looking for food in the air.

My eyes perk up because I see my first clue. I take out my magnifying glass from my suitcase like Sherlock Holmes and there on the shirt, a logo. Many in the picture wore these shirts. Brent didn't wear one, about five people did. I thought I saw a Lowe's here in Seabrook. So I Google Lowe's Hardware store in Seabrook, NH and the search returned with its answer. It seemed like it was in neon lights

LOWE'S OF SEABROOK, NH - Store #1979 and I pause.

The address reads 417 Lafayette Rd., Seabrook, NH and it gave a phone number. I paused, then checked the time on my watch to see if it was a good time to call. It was 3 pm EST so I decided to call 603-760-4019. The phone starts ringing and a woman's voice said, "Seabrook Lowe's, can I help you?"

I paused and said, "Hi there, I'm Marc and I was calling to see if you know of a Brent Brooks?" She paused to almost yell "Yes." Then her voice went calmly, "He doesn't work here anymore. I soon as I heard the word "more" my intuition processed.

"Okay, well thank you for your time." I looked around the room and it was starting to look a lot like my desk in Norfolk, Virginia, papers scattered on the floor and bed of clues in Seabrook.

My thought patterned started to turn. Anyone who wins a Lottery, they're not going to go back to their jobs. They now have a new life and purpose.

I put myself in his shoes, would I go, back to the newspaper if I won the Lottery? The answer came into my head in about two minutes. No, I would go back but I would help the newspaper with stories. Kind of like a newspaper vigilante reporter. I'd have a nickname and all.

Back to the case at hand. . . I decided I needed to drive to Lowe's and talk with some of the employees at Lowe's, maybe someone there can help me with some information toward finding Brent, the Lottery winner of New Hampshire.

I was hungryso I wanted to grab something to eat. I would ask the front desk if they can give me a good place to eat nearby. She said there a was a Wendy's not too far from here. I said thank you and have a good day.

Went to Wendy's, came back to the Hotel to relax a bit. I decided to head out in the morning for a fresh start.

Later that night I hear my phone in my room. I thought who knows I'm here, only my managing editor and wife. By the third ring I decide to pick the phone and there was silence on the phone. I kept saying "Hello, Hello", no one answered back. I waited for a few seconds to hear if someone mightspeak, but there was still a void on the other end of the phone. I hang up and immediately I panicked and thought something must be wrong. I thought, let me call home to Virginia. The phone, rings then my wife's voice comes on and I say "Dear are, you okay?"

"Did you just call me? " Sundara said no she did not call. "That's weird, Marc. Someone knows you're there or it was a miss dial."

Marc responded back, "I got worried that's why I called."

"Nope honey I'm okay," remarked Sundara.

"How's our daughter, honey?"

"She's fine Marc."

"Okay, I spoke slowly. "Okay. I wish you were here in New Hampshire, Sundara. You would like the weather here too, it's like Virginia in some ways." I decided to tell Sundara the location for tomorrow, so she will know where I am.

"I have to go to the Lowe's Department store to find out more information on Lottery winner. I found out his name is Brent Brooks…"Really." Yes, I'm not sure if anyone is going to tell me anything when I get there. But I have to try…"

 "Okay Marc, go find out what's needed. We will be here waiting for you to come home. Love you Husband, will talk to you to tomorrow."

" Okay, Mrs. Dazet.

Chapter 3

My alarm wakes me up at 8 am in the morning … I put it on snooze, but decide immediately to wake up thinking about the reason why I'm here. I start to get ready and decided to grab some continental breakfast from in the hotel near the lobby. I was dressed very casually to fit the Lowe's setting.

As I was walking through the entrance where the breakfast was being hosted, I stood in the room and said WOW to myself and out loud, two Wow's!

They had everything spread out on the breakfast table. I was wishing I had more time to eat everything they had. There were sliced bread and butter with jam and honey, cheese, croissants, pastries, rolls, fruit juice, and various hot beverages. All

I wanted was some hot coffee and two croissants with butter and jam. I would have taken a picture and sent it to my wife, but I thought others would think me awkward, taking a picture of the Mega Universal Breakfast.

After I was done with eating breakfast. I went outside to where my rental car was parked. Fortunately, the car had a cool GPS system. I put into the system 417 Lafayette Rd., Seabrook, NH. When looking at the screen I noticed there was a Seabrook, Texas. I made sure it showed me New Hampshire. The lady's voice said WOULD YOU LIKE TO BEGIN NAVIGATION, then she said PLEASE DRIVE THE HIGHLIGHTED ROUTE.

It was 15 miles from the hotel…I followed the route that the GPS was telling me to,

Made it to the parking lot at about 10 am in the morning, not many cars were in the lot …which is okay. I was thinking that with the store not being too crowded it would give me a chance to talk to Brent Brook instead of him being busy…As I was walking in I saw a cardboard life-size picture of Jimmie Johnson #48. I am a secret NASCAR fan which I basically kept to myself other than my family. I went to my first race in Richmond, VA. When you see race car drivers landing near the race track in helicopters and watching others having fun barbecuing before the race and interacting, you could feel the excitement in the air. That was it for me, I was hooked on NASCAR.

Entering Lowe's the person who greeted me waves and says "Hi, Welcome to Seabrook Lowe's."

I say "Hi" to her and give her the thumbs up. This place is absolutely massive!! All stores seem like an indoor football field in comparison to this.

I started walking and I see the dark bluevested employees walking around.

My thoughts, where to start? I received a text from Amelia, our managing editor while I was walking in the middle of the store. I sent a text back, "On the story now, talk later".

I was thinking, okay "Which department in Lowe's would Brent Brook work in?" I walked down the aisles. Electrical, Appliances and Home Decor, I thought... umm I'm going to go to the painting department first. There were always lots of people who ask questions about painting and paint colors.

When I find the paint department, I see an employee named Richie As I was approaching I kept staring at the new style of paints on the shelves. I turn to the Richie and say "Hello there!"

He said, "Hello, welcome to the Lowe's Painting Department."

"Thanks. One quick question."

 He said, "Sure."

" Do you know a person named Brent?"

He said, "Yes, I do. He worked in the building supplies department, but he doesn't work here anymore".

I said in a low voice, "yes". The clues worked…

Richie said, "Did you say anything, another question?"

Then he stops talking, cold turkey. As if he went into protection mode.

 I said, "Thank you. By the way, what is the best quality of paint on the market."

 He said, There are many. "The one that comes to mind is Behr Interior & Exterior Paint."

 I thanked him again and started to speed walk out of the painting department quickly to the building supplies section. Before I reach the department I am wondering why Richie from the paint department clammed up when I began to inquire about Brent Brooks. Just seemed kind of odd to me, after all, he was an ex-employee who had hit the lottery big time. You would think his fellow employees would be thrilled for him. Well, who knows?

While I'm there in no time, I see a lot of lumber and concrete items. I noticed a person drifting around the area. I walk toward him and he turns around and says "May I help you, Sir"? I notice another Lowe's name tag, this time it said Jack.

I told him I was just in the painting department talking with Richie. He told me that Brent worked in this department. Jack replied,   "Yes, he did. They moved me here two days ago, I use to work in the plumbing department", he said. "Now I'm here." I asked him if he knew where I could find him. He told me he didn't know much, he overheard others talking, saying that he liked to go fishing a lot with his son at the Hampton State Pier near the Seabrook Bridge.

I thanked Jack, he nodded his head back, "Sorry I couldn't be of more help to you."

"No worries," I remarked and wished him a good day.

My second lead happened. Thinking to myself, I'm going to need a fishing hat, so I went ahead, bought a painting hat to fit me as a fisherman. Glancing at my watch I notice that it is only 10:45 am so maybe I can catch them at the pier. My walking turns into speed walking again through Lowe's. Once outside I start to sprint, jumped in the car and made sure I put the right address in the GPS from my phone.

When I put the address in it reads back State Pier Lobster Pound 1 Ocean Blvd…17 miles and I punched it. Without getting into trouble, while I was driving, I pulled out the newspaper that had a picture of Brent when he won the lottery. I just kept studying the picture to get a good mental image while I'm in the car, I'm driving the speed limit I think? It took me 25 minutes to get there, I put on the painting hat, took my shirt out, put some sand in my hands and was ready to go, grabbing the newspaper to take along with me.

As I was walking down the Pier, I noticed the surrounding organization of things. I've been on many piers, we have a couple in Virginia Beach. I was walking slowly as if I was lost, but steady, looking for the same image as the newspaper. I look to the left and right as others are throwing their fishing hooks into the Atlantic Ocean.

I'm walking, looking around and I see almost at the end of Pier Three people dressed in fishing clothes, sitting down on a bench in the middle of the pier. I can make out Brent Brooks and his son just like Jack mentioned at Lowe's. I stare at the man dressed in a black sporting jacket, he looked like a bodyguard. I thought, yes, he would be Brent's bodyguard. This made total sense to me.

I decided to walk over to the man in black and introduce myself. "Hello".

He stood up quickly in an alert stance as I repeated, "Hello, My name Marc Dazet. I work for the *Virginia Pilot Newspaper* in Norfolk, Virginia." I showed him my badge from the paper; he took it from my hands and read it…then he said to me "wait right here". I did what he said as he took my badge and walked over to Brent and his son. I couldn't hear what they were saying, but he gave him my badge. Then Brent and the bodyguard walked over to me to confront me.He said, "Why yes, my name is Brent, how can I help you?"

I paused, then began my story. I told him I flew by airplane from Virginia to hopefully interview him about the Lottery win and what you said about giving.He stopped me and looked around the Pier to see who was watching. Then Brent went on to say, "I can't talk here in the open. Can we talk at my home in the morning?" I told him my flight leaves at 6 pm tomorrow night. Brent handed me a slip of paper and replied, "That will be fine, how about 10:30 in morning?" "Sure." I took out a notepad and pen and gave it to his bodyguard to write the address.

The bodyguard handed the notepad to Brent and he wrote

down the address. Brent handed me the notepad as if he trusted me a little and said: "Talk with you in morning". The whole time we were talking, his son in the background kept fishing.

I took the paper and shook his hand. "Thank you", I replied and on the paper read 32 Hudson Street, Seabrook, New Hampshire.

The bodyguard watched every second almost to say I dare to do something to Brent. I made sure the handshake was stern and quick. And I walked away quickly to make sure no one changed their mind.

I jumped in my car and went back to the hotel with a smile and thankful for all the work and luck on my side at this moment.

Back at the hotel room, the first thing I did is call my office to speak with Amelia. I told her I have an interview in the morning and she was very excited. "This is great," she said. "Make sure you're on that plane tomorrow night Marc with the story. I promised I would and then hung up … and I just paused in the room thinking – What a day!

It's morning now and I start to get ready. I went downstairs to the breakfast buffet. I could not pass on just seeing the breakfast surroundings which could be on "Ripley's Believe or Not". I grabbed my usual two croissants with the works and coffee and headed to the Chevrolet Malibu. While I'm walking to the car I call my wife to check in. It's ringing then I hear the voice I know all too well, "Hi Sundara!"

Her voice sounded happy on the phone, "Hi Honey."

"I will be leaving this evening to come back to Virginia. How's the home base doing?"

"I'm doing okay and your daughter, she's extremely restless. She's her father's daughter for sure Marc, her genes you know."

Marc paused before he said his next sentence. "I know, every time I leave on a newspaper trip she can be this way. I rarely leave the state of Virginia for a story, when I read this story I couldn't pass on the chance to write about it."

"I had more progress here rather than trying to arrange a meeting via telephone. Today I'm meeting Brent at his house this morning for an interview."

"Really"?

"Yes."

"Please be careful Marc, I want you home safe."

While chatting with my wife, I noticed someone in the hotel parking area staring at me from their car. I told Saundra," Honey, I have to go, love you and give Laura a hug from me." I had planned on calling home before I'm on the airplane."Okay Mr. Dazet, talk to you later Honey Bunches of Oats." I smiled and was nervous at the same time because of what I saw in the parking lot.

The person in the car had a hat on and their car was still running. All of a sudden my mind seemed like it drifted. Then I shook my head as if I were clearing out an unwanted vision and immediately returned back to my car and got in to be a bit safer. Then I saw the car and the person punch their gas in what seemed to be a different type of car I had never seen before, then poof they were gone.

I opened my car door and jumped out and just stood up on my feet thinking whoa...what was that…? I got myself together, got back in the car and regained my composure. I put in the address for the GPS; 32 Hudson Street Seabrook, New Hampshire. I noticed it was not that far, about 15 minutes from here in a car so I started driving.

As I was driving down the road, I began to notice the homes seemed to grow from small to large. I was thinking, "Wow, he must have bought a new home with the winnings. Wait a minute, he just won the lottery two days ago. How could he have purchased a new home that quick?" I jump to conclusions too quickly as a reporter. This is just part of the job, always thinking ahead, trying to put the pieces of a puzzle together. Sometimes my instincts are spot-on and other times I am a bit off. My brain is now churning, playing out different scenarios. Bodyguard? New, expensive home? How did he get that money so quick? I will have to be careful on how I pose my questions.I get closer to his home and I was really amazed at the beach homes here in New Hampshire, so different than Virginia Beach, but in a sense the same. I'm driving and then I get to a gate with a device that has codes on the left-hand side. I paused a little and then I heard a female voice."Yes, can I help you?"

"My name in Marc Dazet, I'm a newspaper reporter from Virginia."

"Oh yes, Brent told me about you yesterday," then she tells me to "Hang on one second, let me get my husband to see if you're the person he spoke to."

She seemed very new at the intercom system, I heard a couple of beeps in the background. The next thing you know I hear the voice of Brent, "Yep, that's him, honey."

Chapter 4

The front gate started moving slowly, I was like "This is cool." I drive up the driveway and see what seems to be a house that only a lottery winner could buy. I was truly amazed. I said to myself "well, they did well." I would have done the same thing if I was in their shoes. I keep thinking how quickly they were able to find a place and move in. The road went around the front of the house, kind of valet parking style for a home.

I'm in front of the home and I see the bodyguard there I saw yesterday at the pier. He seems on his toes and watched every move as my car came to a stop in front of the house. I take my notepad, recorder, and the newspaper clippings with me and plenty of pens…oh yes, and my phone just in case I have to call 911.

The bodyguard welcomed me there saying, "We meet again newspaper man".

"Yes, we do," I replied as I asked him how his day was. He didn't answer, he just smiled as he escorted me inside safely.

I was happy to have made it inside to talk to for the first time in my life a lottery winner from New Hampshire. As we came through the front door, there were two more doors that folded open to their house, nice doors, I guessed they were French doors. Then I was in the foyer greeted by two people. One was Brent and a woman who I assumed was his wife. They were sending off warm vibes so I said "Good Morning".

"Good Morning" they replied in unison. There was a tone of excitement in their voices, it seemed like two children when they spoke. "Welcome to our home."

 "I really like the layout, elegant with an ocean feel to it," I replied.

Then Brent paused and had his right hand out to his wife and he spoke: "this is my wife Margret." She looked up at me and said: "Nice to meet you." I reached over to shake her hand and returned the gesture by saying nice to meet you as well. Their bodyguard was in the same room watching everything like a hawk.

I paused, remembering the picture from the newspaper, I didn't see her in the picture I thought to myself. Brent and his wife gave me a brief tour of a smaller area. I followed them around like a puppy and I see moving boxes all over.

"Yes," Brent went on to say, "we have boxes here and still at our old place. We still have a long way to go as you see. Margret asked if I wanted something to drink, coffee or tea and I opted for a cup of coffee, a reporter's favorite beverage in the morning.

Brent turned to me and said, "Let's talk in my office and please excuse the boxes" We walked into an office which seemed like the size of my condo in Virginia Beach and he offers me a seat. The bodyguard shows up all of a sudden, to keep tabs on me for sure. I looked out of the corner of my eye, making sure I was safe and thinking who knows if he has any weapons on him or not. Brent tells the bodyguard he is fine and tells him he can leave.

Brent shuts the door to his office to make the interview more private. I thought he must have something to say privately. I get my items out, my recorder and ask do you mind if I have a recorder on and he said sure. I have my pen and notepad out also and I began the interview.

"Thank You for allowing me the interview and congratulations for winnings."

Yes, thank you. I'm still in shock that actually won. To be honest, this is all so new to me. But I love it. My life is starting to change a lot. New people, I've never met approached me, the phone calls, I'm speechless…It was getting out of hand, though. We're a small beach town here so the word spreads quickly."

I went on to ask, "You won two days ago and you're in a new house already. That was quick."

"Well, the newspaper waited to report the story for security reasons on my behalf. We won the lottery many weeks ago, but they printed the picture two days ago."

"I see, I think that was nice of them to do that for you and your privacy," I replied.

Brent went on to ask, "You flew all the way from Virginia to cover a news story. Aren't there many people who win lotteries in Virginia and all over? Why me?"

"It's a long story Brent, how I have come to be here now. The shorter version being that I randomly choose a newspaper every Thursday from a different area other than Virginia and I happened to choose *The Laconia Daily Sun* here in New Hampshire and you were on the front page as the winner of the lottery. What grabbed my attention is that you went on to say that you planned on using the money to give future generations of your family a chance of having a comfortable life, and this why I flew all the way from Virginia to ask this question, your reason for this."

He said, "Oh, I see." I checked to see if my recorder is on and just waited for the answer. "Have you heard of the Free State Project here in New Hampshire?"

I said, "No I never heard about it."

"Well, it started on September 1, 2001. The goal of the project was to bring 20,000 thousand people to move to a single low populated state. You have to sign a statement that you plan on moving here. The role of the project is to exert the most practical way toward creating communities for the protection of life, liberty, and property."

I was stunned to hear what he said and he kept on. "Here we wanted to help others expand individual rights and free markets … I'm from here in Seabrook. I was born here, my father and grandfather also and when this happened in 2001, the Free State Project, I said to myself I want this for future families in our line."

Just then Brent asked me if I would turn off the recorder. I didn't want to but I respected his request. I said sure I turned off the recorder.

"What I'm about to say needn't be in the newspaper." He went on to say, "Before this, I worked at Lowe's. I learned a lot working there, seeing what other customers bought and receiving while giving me advice. There was a customer who always talked about the satellite he bought and he told me it was expensive to buy, I wrote down the model and I told myself one day I'm going buy this and add this to my house and it happened, out of the blue, I won the lottery and that was the first thing I bought. It's the KVH 01-0369-07 TracVision TV and it supports multiple receivers."

"I had someone install the satellite on my home here. My wife thought I was crazy …It has a remote control where you can point it in any direction and it picks up all channels. One night I pointed the satellite coordinates in the directions my Uncle gave me and his voice went low and the sounds as he explained what happened seemed frightening. This channel showed me an ocean navigational channel markers both red and green and then the camera went below the ocean. In the left side, it read Triangulum Galaxy and I saw these machines I had never seen before in my life below the sea."

His face went pale and I went pale too. Then the channel shut off…then I froze again. I said to myself whose your Uncle?

I knew this was my window to exit the premises. I went on to say "Thank you for telling me about the Free State Project. And I said, "What you told me after that will not leave this room."

All of sudden I hear a knock on the door and there was the bodyguard checking in. "Is everything okay Mr. Brooks?" Brent nodded to the bodyguard and asked him to now leave the door open.

I stood up and reached over to shake hands, paused and I started walking slowly towards the door then all of sudden I turned around and said "Mr.

Brooks, could I have your telephone number just in case I have more questions about the story?"

He said sure, "It's 603-236-7876."

 I wrote it down in my notepad and said "Thank you for letting me talk with you, sir. It's been very intriguing, to say the least."

He nodded yes … I said, "Well I better be heading back to Virginia."

As I was walking back to the foyer, I see the bodyguard from the corner of my eye appear and I see something cool. His son on the fishing pier had a double person, yep that's what I see. I had to rub both eyes to see if I was blurred, I look again and yep sure as real, I see twins boys, they did not see me but I saw them as I was walking out.

I was greeted by Margret and she said, "Thank you for coming here to interview my husband."

I said, "It was great to be here and I wished them much happiness." I shook her hand and walked through the double door. As I was walking to my car the bodyguard gave me a piercing stare and waved. I waved back, jumped into my car and started driving towards the gated exit …the gate opened slowly and I drove through heading back to the Holiday Inn Express.

I keep telling myself "What a trip this has been, three days felt like five." It was around 3:30 pm in the afternoon when I told myself I need to pack and go straight to the airport. I had some weird things happen to be me at the hotel parking garage with people staring at me. I didn't want to chance losing my material.

Chapter 5

I'm on the airplane heading back to Hampton Roads, Virginia from New Hampshire. The airplane flight seemed like seconds and I was back home driving from the airport to Virginia Beach, I called Sundara and I told her I was back and on my way home. I'm on the expressway going towards the beach.

She asked, "Did everything work out for you on the trip?"

I said with caution and an assured voice, "Yes they did…there is a lot I have to tell you, honey."

When I smell the ocean waters I know I'm close to home. I pull into my condo parking lot, grab my material and head up to my condo. My wife was there, waiting for me. When I grabbed the door handle it opened instantly to a hug from Sundara, which was one of the reasons I married her in the first place. I see my daughter Laura dart towards my leg and gripped for a hug. I hugged them both and told them how I missed the both of them.

I gave my daughter a t-shirt and salt water taffy from New Hampshire, she was so happy. I decided to sit down a while being a bit exhausted from the tripped I wished for. All of a sudden the phone is ringing and I see it's around 8:20 pm. The call is from my managing editor at the newspaper.

"You made it back in time", replied Amelia.

"Yes Amelia, I made back. We'll talk soon by phone when my vacation is over. I will make sure I send in the story."

" Okay, text me or call me if you need me. See ya you in a couple days."

 "Okay," I said as I hang up my smartphone

I'm just happy to be home I tell myself. Sundara made a great meal with broccoli, meatloaf, and mashed potato along with some Zum-Zea Tea, it was a great dinner…as the night came upon us quickly.

 I rested because we were heading out to Chincoteague Island here in Virginia for our family vacation. We are going stay for a couple days to relax, ride horses on the beach and just do nothing. The island is not too far from where we are located. I saw a TV show about the Island on the

 Go Flavor Go TV Channel as my wife and I was packing. Our room door was shut so I asked her in low voice, "Have you ever heard of the Triangulum Galaxy?"

She froze and dropped the cup of Zum-Zea tea on the ground and said to me in a surprisingly low voice, "Where did you hear those two words?"

It's a long story, Honey." I decided to stop talking because my wife seemed nervous after I mentioned the Triangulum Galaxy. I quickly tried to change the subject to our vacation but it was too late. Her mind went to those two words I said.

"Marc."

 "Yes," I said.

She asks again like a detective, "Where did you hear that before?"

"Listen, honey, let's get out here on vacation. I promise I will tell you more while we're on our trip." "Okay Marc, that's fine for now, you must tell me soon honey, okay?

I replied back by putting two thumbs up in the air.

We rested but my wife couldn't sleep. The morning arrived without our permission. Everyone seemed excited about our vacation time, my daughter was happy to get away, she grabs her suitcase and we head to my Jeep and put our items on top of the Jeep roof rack. I kiss my wife and we're all in, ready to go. We needed this trip, I can relax without working too much. This time I'm with my family . . . on Chincoteague Island, you can ride bikes, go boating, fishing, and they have a great Farmers market. For my daughter there is arcades and putt, putt golf. This is one of the many reasons we wanted to have a vacation here.

Something unknown to many, there's a flight center there. Yes, the NASA Wallops Flight Center where they launch space projects is located on the eastern shores of Virginia. I was hoping I could see an event happen while we are on vacation. I know we're here for R and R (Rest and Relaxation).

My wife still has that blank stare about our talk last night, she's physically here but not mentally here. She keeps looking at me, then she turns away and I just smile and put on some music to possibly put us in good spirits. Laura in the back so happy for the trip she is dancing in the car sitting down as we get closer to the resort we are staying at. I never turn on the heat in the Jeep, it stayed warm inside for all three of us...I tell myself I love my wife dearly.

A 10-mile road trip, great on gas, and scenery, We check-in and go straight to
the beach. Looking and smelling the ocean, a 7th wonder. My thoughts drifted
to New Hampshire and Mr. Brooks on what he saw on the Satellite channel, and
I know from here on out my life is about to change. As a reporter, you write and
report many stories both good and bad, intriguing, but this one different.

Chapter 6

It's hidden secrets about my own family I have kept from the public and it's about events where if I do not tell the right people, all kinds of forces can happen. My life is about to change Mr. Marc Dazet.

They have so much energy these two, my wife and daughter. We rode horses on the beach. I forgot how fast they were and the strength these animals contain and they're humble about it. All three of us, we love horses, period. I wish I could bring them back with us to Virginia Beach.

Between jumping around the island, I managed to get some typing in for the story. I noticed when I was writing about Brent Brook in Seabrook, New Hampshire, I was dazed from the last statement he made about the Ocean Navigational Markers. I stared out of our ocean view window at the resort hotel room and my thoughts drifted thinking, "What's going on here?"

 I remember thinking one of the reporters at the paper wrote a story about the ocean's future, a new source of energy for the earth. I remember the header "Ocean Energy Turbine". It went on to say this would help bring energy to towns and cities. And how others who are working are protecting the ocean and turbine from projected hurricane damage. "Blue energy" . Marc was looking at the ocean waves thinking to himself, there's a lot going on under the water.

Marc came back to reality from daydreaming to focus on the story he was about to write.

I decide to call Mr. Brooks to ask more questions. I wrote on my notepad some questions I thought would be important to ask. Then I was ready, I started dialing and the phone rang several times and a younger male voice answered. " Hello, who's there?" The voice sounded like a younger version of Brent on the phone.

"Hello, yes, my name Marc Dazet from the *Virginia Pilot*. How are you doing? Can I speak with your father?" I said.

"One second, let me go get him." A pause, then Brent picks up another phone in another room and thanks his son, "Hello, Marc, is that you?"

I responded hearing the older Brent come to the line. "Hi there, how are you doing? I wanted to ask a few more questions, if I may, about the first part of the interview we had?"

Brent got that right away when I said the first part of the interview. I went on to say, "You mentioned a few reasons for giving future generations shares of the lottery. My understanding leads me to believe that this is connected with the Free State Project.was this one of the major reasons?"

And I paused to hear what he was going say back on the phone.. and he said, "Yes, and what I saw on my TV, I decided right then and there I better look out for my family now and in the future, I have twin boys to think about."

I told Brent that I had seen them at the house when I was there last time.

Brent went on to say, "Yes, their names are Jarid and Jarvis, they're only 15 years old. I thought in the future they're going need all the help they can get and pass the funds to them and three more generations after them. This would help our family name stay rooted and somewhat prepared." I sat there in the hotel room thinking. Brent must know something about the future that most of us were not privy too. He knows more than most, and my pen was writing it. I did not stop to think it just wrote.

More words flowed from New Hampshire. "I know I'm giving away something I can use now. I thought of taking the lump sum amount of the lottery winnings now and setting up bank accounts in secret years to be released and it was the advice of my uncle who told me I should do this. We have plenty of funds for our family now. I divided the funds in five ways."

All of sudden I hear an electronic sound at the hotel door, the door movement went in and I recognized the laughter right away. With the movement not seen by many when they entered the door to the hotel room. I cut my conversation short with Mr. Brooks, not revealing too much to my own family about the story I'm about to write for the paper.

I said, "Okay Mr. Brooks, we need to talk again soon."

He said "Yes Marc, this is true and the best to your family" and I said the same back.

My wife froze as she opened the door, staring at me with a quizzical look on her face. "Is everything okay?"

"Yes, all is okay honey." I took my notepad and went over the notes quickly to see what I had written down to make sure all the corrections and facts were okay. I was thinking I have to remember, I'm on vacation and my thoughts are everywhere and Sundara knew this instantly.

It was time for dinner so we decided to try a local seafood restaurant named Captain Zack's Seafood. Laura came into the room to show us her seashell collection.

I noticed Laura had a small cut on her hand from the seashells she was picking up. I pointed this out to her and it was but a half a second and the cut vanished in two seconds. I stared in the air with a blank expression.While we were all getting ready, I happened to look at my phone sitting on the desk in the room and I hear a beep. It was a text coming in. I walked over to the desk to see who this is. The text read, "How's the story coming along? From you know who, Amelia." I text backed, "Going good, I'll be ready to turn the story in tomorrow. I'll send it by email."

I looked at my text messenger section to see if more texts were coming through. I think about five minutes went by with nothing so I sat my phone back on the desk. 1937 As I was walking away I hear another beep, whereas I made a diagonal turn back to the phone. I see the words..."There was a man here looking for you Marc." First, three letter word that came to mind is "Why?"

Instead, I replied back, "Really." The text read on "He wasn't much for words. It seemed like when I was talking to him, I forgot my own name at times. It felt weird. Amelia went on, "He left a business card for you."

Taking in the words written again, I have another thought where I have stored my who, what, and when file. I went on to say "Thank you for the text. There's a lot going on

Amelia… I'll turn in the story tomorrow morning. Bye for now." Then I noticed the last three letters "BFN". (Before Noon)

We had a great time at the restaurant. I noticed at seafood restaurants the eating etiquette vanishes. Those who like snow crab legs or King crab legs, even Alaskan Crab legs, it's great seeing others being themselves when seafood is around. All of us had a great time. My wife and daughter would rank in the category as newbies when it comes to seafood, I'm always teaching. And sharing my knowledge of how to eat a variety of foods we have today from the ocean. Both my wife and daughter look at me like I'm insane when I'm explaining what a crawfish is and how to eat them. It's stressful and entertaining at the same time. We all loved everything on what the ocean offers.

We head back to the hotel and sleep starts to shadow me all of sudden. Those two were still up giggling from having a good time and talking about the Captain Zack's Seafood selections.

I wake up about 8 pm and decide to write the story…

I write the headline: **New Hampshire Pays It Forward**

Then I wrote my story. It took me about two hours to write, I did my spell check, and gave it to my wife to read. She studied it with intent eyes and looked at me and said: "WOW, he is?"

"Yes, he decided to do this with his family."

She started shaking her head and gave me a hug right away. She said, "This is why I like the human race and why I came here." I stared back and shook my head to understand what she said. She went on to say she wished Virginia would have the Free State Project.

"Maybe in the future," I said. "It gives us something to hope for."

I emailed Amelia, clicking enter on my laptop to send the copy. I was happy it was done. Wishing I could write more insights from the northeastern state. My wife and daughter wanted to walk on the beach just before sunset settled in, to take in the ocean and fresh air as we often do when we're near water.

Sundara tells me she's proud of me for writing a great story. I think of Laura and the future. We get back to the room and start packing, getting ready to leave for Virginia Beach in morning.

I was folding my clothes in the room for my suitcase, Sundara scoots near me, whispering in low voice in her native dialect. She goes on to say "Marc I have to tell you something that's within me because you're my husband. She goes on to say, "the Triangulum Galaxy has been our enemy for many caducities."

Marc knew this word to mean "years".

Those who come from there are intelligent and have adroitness in telepathic powers, they can mentally receive and can counter emotions and restrict the moment of other minds, understand all languages and allows others minds to speak to others and show each other what they're thinking. The whole time she was speaking I stared into the abyss and took it all in and my thoughts permanently went foggy. Then she stopped talking and walked out of the hotel room as she was taking a breath from telling something that no one knows.

As I stood there in the room by myself ..I couldn't help but think about the business cards handed to Amelia.

They may have been from these people. Or when I was followed in New Hampshire, the same pattern here. Time would only tell the truth.

Chapter 7

It's early in the morning and were all packing, still happy from our vacation on Chincoteague Island. My wife and daughter are ready to head home to Virginia Beach. I am too, to find out the answers. Some of what my wife told me and the business card that was handed to Amelia.

At the hotel check-out desk, I thanked the hotel manager on what a great stay we had. "I hope you can return soon," he said and waved goodbye as we left the hotel.

We walked to the Jeep slowly, wanting to leave and stay at the same time. We're driving back and I put on the song *Message in the Bottle by Sting* as it could have a meaning for me now. We all sing the song, even my daughter, real loud as we head back to Hampton Roads.

Meanwhile, in Fort Riley, Kansas, Second Lieutenant Harold Johnson receives a call. He picks up the phone and there on the other end is Colonel Mathews, "Hello 2LT. How are you doing?"

 "Sir, I'm doing fine. Sir.""Could you be in my office at 1500 hours. I have something to tell you."

The Army Officer said he would be there and hung up the phone. LT Johnson wondered about the meeting with the Colonel. The time is 4:55 pm in Kansas and the horns on base are about to sound, telling everyone that it is 5 pm on the base.

The commander of the division, 2LT Harold Johnson stands up and walks over to the second in command's office to tell him he would out of the office at 3:00 pm and to handle any problems that would arise. "Please text if you have any problems, Sage, okay."

Sage, second in command, was in the Army but wanted to be in the Air Force. That's all he talked about to his commanding officer. Flying. He trusted Sage to handle everything while he was away at the meeting tomorrow.

Harold started toward home in their Mazda CX 3 SUV, he needs the room for his family. Driving home is not too far living on the base in officers housing.

As he arrived home, he was greeted by his wife Hannah Johnson and children, which were grounded upstairs. Hannah goes on to say that Zelda and Nolan are in the rooms for acting up.

Harold asked "What did they do? Hannah said, "I called for them to come in for supper, no answer. Finally an hour later they come in. I told them no Internet or phone till tomorrow.

Harold agreed with her completely, he went upstairs to his children's room and to say "Hello". As he opened their door he was greeted by two sad faces. Harold said, "You guys need to listen to your mother when she's calling for you for supper. If you want to chat with your friends on the internet, make it in on time for dinner."

Zelda looks at her father and said, "No internet, I'll make sure I'm in at 4:30 pm Dad from here on out" Harold, being the father said that's a good idea. Nolan, his son agreed. The family was at the dinner table eating and before they started eating, Harold asked his son to say grace and he did, This is something that the Johnson family likes and that's eating good food. Hannah cooked Lasagna and Garlic bread with salad as well, and it was the best.

While we were eating, Harold made an oath with himself not to bring work home. Sometimes the high stress of being in the Army comes out, but all in all, Harold was able to keep work at work and home at home. In the middle of dinner Harold turned to Zelda and Nolan and said, "Look, I talked it over with your Mother tonight and asked if we can play a board game since there is an internet ban for this evening, along with no TV. I thought this might be the time to introduce you to board games your mother and I grew up playing."

Both of them looked at each other as if their father was speaking Japanese. Harold continued, "Yes a classic board for our family... Family town hall in the living room at 1900 hours." Nolan started counting on his hands what 1900 hours mean.

 Nolan said, "Okay at 7 pm"."Yes at 7 pm. And bring your wits with you…!" Hannah and Harold have collected board games for many years. Before there was the internet on the planet they had Yahtzee, Monopoly, Candy Land, Sorry, and even Operation. Harold and Hannah had kept them in good shape for this very moment. Tonight both Harold and his wife were going to see if their children had that competitive gene in them. Both Harold and Hannah were extremely competitive when it came to playing games. "Go for the Gusto" was the Johnson motto!

The game being playing tonight is called "Sorry". Harold thought the name fit the occasion for his wife scolding them for not coming home on time for dinner. Yep, the lesson was gonna taught by a classic board game.

Let me explain the game "Sorry" First, you must choose four pieces of the same color. Then place these pieces on ponds on the board that matches your color on the game board, then grab the deck of cards and shuffle them. Choose a player to go first, then it goes in clockwise, the drawing. Now to move your piece out of the pond and onto the track, think of it like a NASCAR race track on the board game...in order for you to get on the track, you must pick a card that has the number 1,2 or a card that says "Sorry" on it. If you don't draw a card that draws your piece out of the pond, you have to skip your turn."

Both Zelda and Nolan are looking at their Dad as he describes the game in full details … Mom has a cool smile." Once you draw one of the three cards, you can move onto the starting circle or the race track if you prefer." The kids nod their heads. "Once you're on the board at anytime you land on a piece that's not yours, you can "BUMP" their piece off the board and they have to start back in their own pond again." They're smiling at Harold the more he tries to explain. "Each card you draw, you move around the board to get into the "Home Space".

"Think of it this way, Zelda. We all have a home base with our own color with four pieces, we have traveled around the board to land inside our home base. And in order to land each piece home, you have to have the correct number to land home…if it takes seven moves to make it home and you draw 5 you must skip your turn until you draw the seven card." They were both amazed at that rule. "Now on the game board/race track," Harold continues, "there are "Slides." If you land on their color slide you can slide your piece down to the end. If other pieces are on that slide, you bump them off the board. And they have to start over.

If your own color lands on your slide, you're not allowed to slide. Again, yell when you have traveled around the board one time."

"To win you have to bring each piece home and get all your pieces into the safety zone then Home Base. Each card tells us what to do during the game, to move forward or backward, some cards can say switch your piece with someone else's piece on the board". The children looked ready to play.

Zelda said, "Let's play."

"One more thing, if you get the Card that says "Sorry" on it, you can take your piece out of the start area and "BUMP" another player's piece off the board and start where they last were."

"I love this game," Hannah yells out…and rubs her hands together like a track runner.With a gleam in her eye, Zelda says, "I'm going to be late for dinner tomorrow too if this is the punishment we get."

Hannah says, "You better not," trying not to crack a smile. Harold covers his smile as they get ready to play.

The Johnson's family battle had begun.! It was great fun, everyone laughed and it took Harold's mind off of what Colonel Mathews was going to say to him in the afternoon. He kept wondering what it is? We played the board game until around 9:30 pm, their bedtime for school. Hannah and Harold stayed up talking for a few hours and Harold told her about what happened today. She was worried and thinking maybe an opportunity was going to- happen.

The entire household was sleeping soundly that night. The next thing you know the alarm clock going off at 7 am in the morning. Harold pops out of bed to get ready and start towards the Army barracks to meet Colonel Mathews.

Driving into the building, Harold notices this building has more security than most of the barracks.

He checks in and is saluted by the soldier and directed to walk through a metal detector. The guard told him to touch what looked like a remote tablet to take my hand prints as I walked forward. Then a soldier said to go to the third floor. An elevator was there and it said "hand print" and 2nd Lt. Johnson touched it and it opened right away.

With such a quickness, the 2nd Lt. thought he had never in his life had seen an elevator like this. He hops in and the elevator took about half a second and Harold was on the third floor.

The door opened and there was another guard in a uniform that was not the same color as the 2nd Lt's.

It had blue with green and purple on it. First time Harold had seen that and he's been in the military for many years. He thought to himself, 'What's going on here.' The guard there said, "Hello 2nd Lt. Johnson."

The Lt. said, "Hello."The guard says, "Colonel Mathews is expecting to see you right away." He nodded his head and moved forward._

As Harold was walking down the hallway, there seemed to be fewer doors than before, which was odd. He kept walking until he came to a door that said, **Colonel Stan Mathews** and on the door, there was more. It read **Unit: The Spaceborne Marine**. Harold paused for a second before opening the door. "Where did this unit come from?" he wondered.

There sitting in the room, a round table with technology devices on it. There were lots of chairs surrounding the table with Colonel Mathews sitting there, the only person there. Just Colonel Mathew and the 2nd Lt.'s mind is racing. "I never knew such a room existed," he thought to himself.Colonel Mathews extended his hand and said, "Hello 2nd Lt Harold Johnson". This hello was different today, more of an astonished greeting today. "Thank you for attending today."

Harold waited before saying anything. Maybe the Colonel would come right out with it, whatever 'it' was.

"I was concerned about our meeting today Colonel."

"Well anytime there's change, there's a concern. You do not have to worry 2nd LT, I have your best interest in mind, I've always had."

"I'm ready, let's go," he replied.

"Have a seat, I want to show you something." Then he hit a button, a screen came down from the ceiling in movie format. Everything in this room seemed new, the chairs, the screen, even the curtains seem futuristic.

The screen came down and stayed blank except for a purple dot that keeps blinking on the bottom of the screen. The Colonel went on talking, "Now for the reason you were called here. The Military has new Infantry units that are divided into three divisions."

the 2nd Lt.'s mind was swirling now but he keeps listening. He said, "We have been monitoring species movement in ocean waters of something we think is not from earth. We have been observing their movements now for many years and they only seem to be in our ocean waters that we know of."

"Our three new infantry units were created from Space Intelligence gathering that we had from satellites and an earth surveillance unit we created in the 1960's.

We have waited till the right time to form these infantry units and now is the time…"

"I have called you here to be a part of one of the three units we're starting. The three units are **The Planetary, Spaceborne, and Planetary Marines Reserves (PMR),** each unit will have the same Motto *"Above and Beyond"."* As he was talking, Harold couldn't believe the words floating in air, he absorbed every word.

"What you're hearing in this room cannot leave the room and you must decide here today if you want this mission." the 2nd Lt. keeps thinking that we're going to have to move from the Kansas base. The Colonel said, "Yes, just like Dorothy, you will have to leave Kansas for this mission and join the new unit we have assigned you to today."

Harold took a deep breath and keep listening. "I'm with you, go on Sir."

The Colonel went on to say, "We have assigned you to the Spaceborne division. This division is combined with the Army, Navy, and Marines. The Planetary Units are combined with the Coast Guard and Air Force units. We handpicked each person for the units. The PMR unit is forces of all units together with secretly skilled personnel involved with the Planetary Marines Reserves…All infantry units will be top secret. Please understand the secrecy and the seriousness of my words 2nd Lt. Harold Johnson.

"Yes, sir, I do understand," he replies.

Colonel Mathews at that moment ended the meeting. The screen that had been pulled down with the purple button was still beeping silently, he tapped a button and the screen went back up and the lights came on automatically. "The next time we meet we will talk about what each unit's responsibilities are. We wanted a short briefing on this matter."

"Are you interested in coming on board 2nd LT?"

"Yes sir, yes."

"We picked you because you have brought with you strong leadership qualities and your test scores in the Army have been good. And you have excellence swimming skills.

Well…there are more reasons why we chose you 2nd LT. Harold Johnson. You're here for a reason, for a mission unheard of…"The 2nd Lt. said, "Yes Sir," with a salute. "I want to be part of this Infantry unit."

"You may leave now and we will be in touch to talk about more."Harold walked out the door with his hand prints on the door. He walked away slowly, it seemed to take longer to leave the building than it did when he entered it. Harold's thoughts were going at a top speed which made him walk slower, trying to think and understand what he had just been told. He finally made it back to his car.

Gripping the steering wheel with both hands to make sure his nervousness did not affect his driving … he took off for home. When Harold arrived home he opened the door to the officers' quarters and Hannah was there. He told her he couldn't speak about the meeting.

"All I can tell you is we are going move," Harold said. Hannah, of course, looked surprised and wanted to know more. He went on to say, "I don't know where but we're about to move my dear wife Hannah.

Chapter 8

Today in Virginia Beach the weather feels brisk and the ocean waves are calm aka low tide. I'm rested up from the vacation and ready to head into the office to speak with Amelia, my managing editor of the *Virginia Pilot*.

Norfolk downtown is always growing, more buildings and entertainment for Hampton Roads as a whole. We have a minor league baseball team called the Norfolk *Tides* and the Waterside District, which is beautiful. In the parking garage, I'm looking around to see if anyone followed me here.

Ever since New Hampshire, I'm always looking around to see if someone is around watching. I walk in the office, greeted by the front desk receptionist.

I walk straight to Amelia's office. "I'm Back, Amelia I'm back, did you miss me?" "Did you get my story by email?"

"Yes Marc, I liked the story a lot. We will run the story tomorrow morning. We wanted you to look it over again to make sure everything is a go."

I was happy, my managing editor liked the story for printing. I shake her hand and start walking out the door, then she said the word "Boomerang."

I turned around and said "Boomerang? What does that mean?" She kind of talking in a riddle format.

So she says, "Many have heard of me, but no one has seen me, and I will not speak back until spoken to, who am I?I looked at Amelia puzzled, I thought about it and I replied, "Let me write this down in my notebook and I'll be back with the answer." I told her.

Hey, remember? I do have a business card for you."

"Oh yeah, I forgot about the card you mentioned to me while I was on vacation." Amelia handed me the card I grabbed it slowly still thinking of her riddle.

While I was walking back to my desk, I noticed the color of the card and it said **Wilkens R.E** and under the name, it reads **Earth Surveillance Unit East Coast.** It was a solid card, not cheap. I thought who is this? I never heard of this unit before so I put the card put in my wallet and said, Thank you for liking my story, Amelia".

" You're welcome, Taking the trip there was a good idea Marc."

 As I was walking to my desk, I thought about the riddle answer and it hit me the answer. I pick up my desk phone to call Amelia she picks up and I say "An Echo" That's the answer to the riddle" Many have heard of me, but no one has seen me, and I will not speak back until spoken to, who am I?" Amelia said, "Yes you got it." She then mentioned she was on the other phone line with a copy editor. talk soon Marc .. "I still can't believe you got that riddle." Amelia responded back.

Back at my desk, I took out the business card. I wanted to see where the area code was from. I looked at the card and it said area code 603, I was thinking that's in New Hampshire, hmm, I think this could have been the person watching me while I was there.

I decided I must call the number. I go outside the building to my car to make the call. I had to put my cell next to my ear and get my notepad with a pen. I start dialing the number 603 743-1313; the phone rings and a voice comes on the phone to say "Hello Marc, I was thinking soon you would call."

How do they know it was me calling? The voice repeated, "Hello Marc."I said "Hello, this is Marc, I received the business card you dropped off at my office. Can you tell me what this is about?"

The voiced spoke again."I'm with a division of the Military called the Earth Surveillance Unit."

 Clueless about this unit, Marc starts writing in his notepad. The voice said, "You were in New Hampshire talking with Brent Brooks, the Lottery winner." I didn't agree with him I just listened. "We picked up a signal that there that was movement in the ocean. We don't know the exact coordinate where the signal was either coming from or going to. Our system picked up something from the water.

I thought to myself about my circle of people, my family and Brent's family in New Hampshire and how I must go into protection mode while I'm on the phone with this person I hardly know. I think to myself , I need to speak to my wife Sundara.

I denied everything he said. He replied back "Look Mr. Dazet, it's okay not to tell me anything, you don't know who I am so that's understandable. Look, keep my card and if you ever want to talk to me about anything suspicious call the number at any time of the day or night, okay? We work to protect the citizens."

"Okay, sir, I will," I stated, "I have to go, thanks for talking." I clicked the talk button to hang up, jumped out my car, ran back to the office to speak to Amelia and ask if I can go, I have an emergency. She said sure, I ran out back to the car and drove home straight home, I didn't call or text. I wanted to talk with my wife at once.

It took me no less than 15 minutes to get back to Virginia Beach, my normal time to travel back home, about 30 to 45 minutes because of the 5 pm traffic. This time I'm not sure of the motivation, but I made into the oceanfront in 15 min. I ran to the condo and told my wife with a hand gesture come with me, I didn't speak, she knew to be silent if I used a hand symbol. That meant for her to follow me into the Jeep, I put my hand on hush signal in the car. I drove to the ocean and fortunately there not many people there. We jump out of the car at the shoreline parking lot and she follows me. As soon as we were on the ocean front shore, I started talking.

Marc looked around to see if anyone was listening. While the ocean waves crashed into the Atlantic. In a whispered tone I say,

"Sundara, someone is following us, and listening to our conversations. A special unit called the Earth Surveillance Unit."

"What Marc?" She replied with a concerned look.

"Amelia at the office gave me a business card and I called the number there. The person knew I was talking with Brent, the lottery winner. He knew that," Marc repeated himself

"Really?" Sundara said.

"Yes." The wind outside the ocean was blowing strong, all of sudden the wind stopped and Sundara started talking. She said, "Okay", then something in a different language, a language I knew but I could not speak it.

"Bgb Jg Mpqy Cdmwt Oeeee." Sundara said, "He did not know about you, Honey."

She went on to say, "QM K Ycc Hccb Vq Eqpvev."

I replied, "Okay, that would be fine, when will you contact them?"

Sundara went on to say, "It will be in two days." and then I suggested we leave the ocean and go home. When we started walking to the car, all of a sudden the wind started back up again where we stood. As we were driving home the both of us were in a silent daze. Thinking somewhere, someone could be listening to us talking in the Jeep.

We arrived home and soon Laura would be home from school. I thought about my trip to New Hampshire and as a newspaper reporter, I had to find out about the Earth Surveillance Unit. I googled them and started typing in the search engine. Curiously, I waited to see and nothing came up. I tried typing the words in many ways and still blank answers. I tried other search engines too like Yahoo and Bing. I was staring at my computer screen, puzzled and thought who would know them and how can I find out more.

I thought Brent told me he had an uncle who works somewhere high up in the government. Maybe he would know. I reached for my phone on my home desk to call. This time Brent answered the phone and I say, "Hello is Brent there?"

 Brent replied back "Who is this?"

"It's me, Marc. From the Groundhog Day movie calling again." Brent laughed right away and said that was a good movie.

"Well Marc, what's going on?" he said.

"Well since I left New Hampshire a lot of things have been going on. I've been followed in your state and at the office here in Virginia, someone gave me a business card from a unit called the Earth Surveillance Unit."

"Wow," Brent said.

"I called to see if your Uncle would know of them?"

Brent said he would have to call him to find out. He went on to ask me to call him back later this week and he would have more information. I replied sure.

I hung up with Brent in New Hampshire.

Just then, my daughter, Laura had come home and I asked her, "How was school?"

"There are some girls at school who keep making fun of me Dad," she replied. I asked her why and she said, "The way I talk, they said I have a funny way of talking. And they keep making fun of me, So for the whole day, I kept the temperature at school for everyone at 40 degrees. Everyone there was wearing coats except me, it was funny."

I sat down in a chair in our living room to explain, I told her not to do that again. "You must be careful where you do that. "Promise me this Laura." She smiled and said okay then went on to have a snack in the kitchen.

Not even a half hour goes by at the condo and the phone rings again. It was Brent on the phone.

"Hello, Marc?"

"Yes, boy that was quick," I remarked.

"I had to call you right back, I got a hold of my Uncle. He said that the Earth Surveillance Unit has something to do with Space. It's a unit that's sent out to investigate local affairs. But they have orders not to be involved in local affairs, just when they catch wind of something extraterrestrial happening in the communities, then they send them out. They're good at deception, you would never know they're around. My uncle told me they're sent to all regions of the states and abroad. And this unit is not new, it's been around for a long time."

As I was listening, my head was spinning like a top.

"This unit is made up of all people. They move quickly, if you see them they want you to see them. If they call there's a good reason to talk with them, they only make themselves known for a really good reason. That's all I got from my Uncle."

"Wow Brent, just who exactly is your Uncle?"

"I don't even know what he does Marc. But he tells me things I never heard of and they come to be true."

"Thank you, Brent, you've helped a lot."

"Anytime Marc, I'm sure, We will be in touch again."

I started thinking again how that unit has been watching me and I wondered how long and when...And how?

Now with everything I'm doing, I need to be more careful from here on out to protect my family. and any info I stumble upon. My wife Sundara keeps staring at the picture in our living room which had stars and it says Andromeda Galaxy. I put my arms arouod her and I asked her if she missed home and she said she missed it terribly.

And we both gave each other a hug, But as I was looking at the picture, I had a flashback of what Brent said and what he saw on the satellite when he discovered the new channel, I thought "Whoa, there's something going on here.

Chapter 9

2nd Lt. Johnson was at home pacing the floor, back and forth and thinking as he does before a big mission, knowing he can't talk about with his family.This is why he joined the Army. He wanted to be his own man. He was the youngest in his family. He admired his older brothers and sister as they grew up and he wanted to take care of his own family and he saw the Army as a way to do this and see the world too. He joined the Army enlisted rank, this means any rank below that of a commissioned officer.

He was on the swim team in high school and he went to school at night to get his degree. His wife, Hannah bet him he couldn't be an officer in the Army and he took that to heart.

He went to night school, then had to have reference letters to apply for Officer Candidate School OSC, a 12-week long program in Fort Bening, Georgia. When finished, he would be commissioned Second Lieutenant (2LT) and today Harold Johnson is proud he took the bet from his wife to become an officer. When people dare him to do something and his wife is in the room, she always warns "do not dare him". Okay, some believe her and others find out on their own.

As he paced the floor with thoughts of what Colonel Mathews said, his wife knew something was bothering him and he said "I promise honey, I will explain soon. I have to go in today for more briefing."

At the briefing office, he went through the same process as the other day. When he reached the room he went to the last time he still had to use his handprint identification. It was still very new to see this type of technology. He went into the room and this time there were two people, the Colonel and a female military person in a new type of fatigue uniform. She stood up, saluted, and sat down.

She said, "Hello (2LT) Johnson, how is your family?"

I said, "Fine but my wife is worried about what's happening." Both the Colonel and the woman remarked that they wanted to explain to all the 'new' families at the same time.

"Colonel Mathews and I want to explain more about the new units and what they're doing. We want you to join the Spaceborne Infantry which

operates in Space and on the ground," remarked the woman.

I thought "space infantry, what?""There will be a one-year training with others who were chosen for this unit, again they are from all branches of the military."

Then she taps a button and the screen that I saw the last time comes down in auto mode. Always a sight to see this happening, I say to myself. I have seen many monitor screens, this one was different the way the screen came down in the middle of the room.

The lights dimmed and there were many small lights blinking in the room. I thought the room was going take off, like a spacecraft. But it didn't. She continued speaking.

"We're sending you to the area we call "The Land Cover Classification" near the ocean." All of sudden on the screen it showed an area, it had several bluish and green domes and it was near the ocean and they were live screen shots. You could see people running in platoons with the same type of uniform fatigues that this lady talking had on.

 My eyes got wide as I looked at her. She continued, "You will learn a lot and see a lot having to do with land, ocean, and space." I nodded my head to show I was listening and my thoughts were spinning but controlled as she kept talking.

"You will learn about various new military armor suits and about rapid deployment forces at this location.

The Spaceborne unit would be the unit sent in for hot zones before the big logistical unit, the (PMR) Planetary Marines Reserves, arrive. This unit is training at different locations. We want you to keep an open mind on what you're learning.

I agreed with my nod again. "We are going to give you a couple of months to talk things over with your family about moving. We'll have more briefings before you go."

All of sudden the screen went back up and in a matter of seconds, the room went back to normal. She and the Colonel stood up to shake my hand and then she said, "This is the last time you're going to see me here. Others will give you more briefings before you go.

I said "Okay".

"We will talk again in the future, I'm one of the designers of this infantry unit". Then she shook the Colonel's hand and walked out and poof, just like that she was gone.

It was me and Colonel Mathews standing there. I said, "Whoa".

He went on to say "You haven't seen nothing yet! Put on your seatbelt (2LT) Johnson". I shook his hand and walked to open the door to head to my car and go home. As I was driving home I thought,

I have to talk with my wife and family.

Chapter 10

In Virginia Beach,, after all that's happened, we had a great dinner and the night
flew by. I woke up about 6 am to see if my story ran in the newspaper column
and there it was with a picture: **New Hampshire Pays it Forward**. I was proud
of my newspaper for the ethics they have on certain stories. I reread the story to
make sure all the details were in there for the reader. I looked over to my wife,
staring at her as she sleeps and started to reminisce on how we met.

Ten years ago…I was studying Journalism at Pepperdine University in Malibu,
California. I minored in atmospheric sciences, and there she was, studying
weather like I was. I always had a thing about the weather in college, our group
of friends hung out together and we watched everything weather on the weather
channel like it was football bowl game. We yelled at the weather person saying
no this or that and awed at the temperature.

They're in class, ten years ago, was Sundara, sitting there learning about the
earth's atmosphere, its processes, and the effects other systems have on the
atmosphere.

I thought the friends I met in college would be keepers because there's not many
people on the planet into weather like I am. When I saw her there, I was hooked
at first sight. This certain day we were outside studying the makeup of clouds
and I said: "What do clouds wear under their shorts?" She stared at me and I
said "Thunderpants." She looked at me and just laughed and I smiled and said
she has a sense of humor and I wanted to get to know her

more. I asked for her name she told me Sundara. I thought to myself, speak Marc speak , "My name Marc Dazet and I'm from Virginia."

My alarm goes off and my thoughts turn back to the present times in our condo at the ocean, I had to get ready for work soon. I daydream too much I told myself, this is why I'm a reporter. I had a bit of time so I made some coffee and just sat at the kitchen table. So many things have happened. What do they have to do with each? It certainly seemed that the recent events were connected, but how?

I take the last gulp of coffee and head out to my Jeep. It's time for a visit to the newspaper office. As I was driving I noticed someone in a silver car, then it disappeared, then I noticed it again in my rear view mirror. "Am I going crazy?" I thought to myself. I shook it off to coincidence and just kept driving.

By the time I reached the office the silver car was gone. I keep thinking about the business card. While, I'm at the office and I say good morning to those around me and go to my office. Posted on my office door I see a piece of paper taped to it. In colorful magic markers it says:

GREAT STORY MARC. VIRGINIA PILOT STAFF.I looked and smiled and told myself, people still do care here in America. I sat down looking at my desk and clicked on my computer, fishing around searching the internet for other possible news stories. I took a look at the weather for the area and other areas. Went to get some coffee and when I came back, on my desk, I see a manila envelope. It was addressed to "M" so I opened the envelope. Inside seemed to be papers that resemble some type of very elaborate blueprints. I see the words Hydrogen and a lot of details to some type of plans. I thought, "What in the world is this."

The plans were in two languages, one I understood, the other wording I had never heard or seen before. They looked like plans for taking or removing hydrogen from the ocean water and a picture of something removing the oxygen bubbles and a huge battery source unit. It stated that the water is made of two elements hydrogen and oxygen. I see another word, electromagnetic. Then it went into another language. To separate the two elements there was a picture of an area with the word salt and there was another word next to salt with many types of pictures and shapes on the blueprints. I saw a word at the end of the blueprint page, Quest Ooynt.

The language I had never seen in my life and I have seen many languages on this planet. This one was different, how it looked and was written. I thought someone wanted hydrogen from the ocean, they're both American and something else. I put the plans back into the envelope and took them with me thinking "Wow. Don't know what this is about but it is definitely worth looking into." The other strange wording didn't look like any type of dialect I had ever seen. But yet, there was something vaguely familiar about it, especially if I tried to pronounce the words as written.

Now I am in panic mode wondering who gave this to me and knew my name. There was a lot there I could work with. The day at work went by fast. I was there, but my mind was somewhere else. I was trying to put all the pieces together of what happened to me or what I know that made some sense and other parts with no comprehension of what's happening. I looked out the window in my office and stared at the clouds, wondering as a reporter, would I want to know more?

I told myself, it's too late, time is moving forward and it wants me to move forward with it. Driving home at the end of the day I texted my wife and asked if she was okay. She texted back yes I'm okay and she was about ready. When Sundara said she was ready I knew what this meant, she is leaving me for a brief moment to find answers. The way she leaves is unexplainable to any beings on earth. I answered okay, then I texted the word "MEET" and she got what I meant. We meet at the shoreline by the ocean again where we are away from people.

I explained to her about the envelope and the ocean hydrogen words

on the blueprint plan. I gave them to her to look at and there was a glimmer of recognition in her eyes. It was like she was making a mental picture of the plans and understood everything on the paperwork I showed her. Just then she looked up and in a low voice says, "I am ready husband."

She kisses me and walks closer to the water. She opened her cell phone and before my eyes, the shape of her cell phone changes and a beam of light, (light green and yellow) came out from the bottom of the cell. She took the phone and put that beam of light on her feet to the top of her head. The beam engulfed Sundara. She says "I love you, honey.

I will be back, take care of Laura. I must go and find what's going on." Then with the beam on, she jumped and ran into the water and she vanished from the water in two seconds, along with the green/yellow beam of light. I stood there shaking like a leaf. I've seen this, the means by which she travels many times . . . but every time she does this, it's always amazing to me. The beam left the phone device and the shape went back to the cell phone she had. I could not see my wife anywhere in the water…I put my head down, looking at the water and then up at the clouds in the sky. I tell myself she better be safe.

Thinking she may be back sooner than she thought, I waited for about ½ hour, nothing. I finally turned the car engine on and drove slowly, looking in the rear view mirror for signs of her coming back. I keep looking, though there are no signs of her appearing. I keep driving home. I thought she'll be back in two days and I need to be home for our daughter as she comes home from school.

Driving back to the condo I see the yellow school bus and I got there just in time. She jumps on the sidewalk and I wave from the car. "Hi, Laura."

She yells back, "Hi Dad, where's Mom?"

"She had to go out of town for a couple days."

Laura always knew something was going on. I could tell by the way she reacted to telling her the news."Is Mom in some type of trouble?"

I told her everything was okay, she just had to go out of town for a day or so and that she would be back soon.

Our daughter knew where her mother went. Laura said, "She went home."

"Yes, she did." I walked in, shut the door and I toss my keys up to catch them in the air and repeated the process while I was staring at the picture on our living room wall that read 'Andromeda Galaxy'.

Chapter 11

I miss my wife Sundara. She has been gone for only one day and I miss her. She has a lot of characteristics that Laura inherited yet she has both of our genes more of Sundara.

I was eating dinner. I do like cooking, we're having beef shanks with mashed potatoes and gravy. I can cook a lot of dishes, my wife knows how to make dishes from Ooynt. As I was eating I started daydreaming again about her and me, and I knew before I married her there was something different about her I was not sure until one day.

We both got a job while in college at a restaurant off campus and we were in the back of the restaurant and both of us somehow we got stuck in the freezer. I mean stuck before the restaurant opened, we came in early to set up and Sundara whispers to me out of the blue, let's go into the freezer, I want to kiss you and I said, "Who me?" pointing to myself. She said,

"Yes, you And I said "Well you don't have to twist my arm," so we both went in the freezer and shut the door. We started kissing in a room where the temperature reads about 38 Degrees Fahrenheit, it was cold. All of a sudden as I was leaning behind the door, I noticed it was closed, but I happened to open the knob to see if the door would open a little bit and it didn't. I stopped my kiss and looked at my watch.

"Whoa, we came in early to study and prepare for work, it's still about 1 hour and ½ before others show up." I texted another person on my phone to see if they're coming in, no text back or phone call back.

We were there for about 45 minutes, then all of sudden the temperature in the freezer got warmer. I looked at her and she looked at me. I started touching my hands and face I couldn't believe it. I asked her,"

"Do you know what just happened in here?" I kind of freaked out a little. Noticing she was not touching her hands and face from the air becoming warmer, she then put one finger on my lips and said: "Shhh, I will tell you more later."

I look at the gauge reading and it said 70 degrees. Who is this person I'm dating? I kept asking what just happened here? It took another ½ hour and someone opened the door and instantly the temperature went back to 32 degrees and I shoot a look at her as the freezer door opened and she threw a wink at me. A staff member was looking at me and I said "Thank you for opening the door" and said "it was freezing in here", crossing my arms and having the shiver symbol. I told them to make sure to check the food to see if it was okay.

I walked out still warm and Sundara and I kept working that day I was still shaking my head at her and I kept her secret safe. I hear my daughter's voice in the background faintly say, "Dad are you okay?"

I look around and it was my daughter sitting across from at the dinner table. I said, "Yes, I'm here, are you okay?"

She said, "Yes, can you pass the salt and pepper?" She went on to say, "I was trying to ask you for awhile now."

"Sorry honey, I was thinking about something and lost my train of thought."

I passed the salt and pepper and she smiled and said: "It's about time."

"Okay, okay. I was thinking about your mother dear."

"Okay, I understand," my daughter replied. We finished up dinner and she talked about school and the people who picked on her stopped picking on her. "They didn't know where the cold air came from when they stopped picking on me, it stopped."

I smiled and said, "You need to be careful about doing that around people."

She said, "Okay, I will". She finished dinner and did her homework. I sat in the living room looking at her cell phone wondering when she was going warn me of her arrival back to Virginia Beach. The lights changed to a different shade of color and I kept thinking this is "IT", I know when it really happens from the last times.

I was looking at Go Flavor Go TV Channel in the living room that evening, then all of sudden I received a text it said "Tomorrow at 3 pm", then one- word "MEET" I read the text and I knew, I just knew…It seems like it's been a month since she's been gone but it was only for two days.

The morning came fast, it was 8 am. I told Amelia by the text I would be in later this afternoon to drop off my work. Amelia, she said that fine. I told her I had another idea for a story that I would tell her about at the office.

I made sure my daughter was safe on the bus to school. I said have a good day and be good and I fatherly high-fived her and she slapped my hand back.

Then after the bus drove away I must have sprinted to the car and drove to the waterfront. I know I was early this day, I wanted to be near the ocean just in case she came in early. I grabbed some breakfast at the Pocahontas Pancake House on Atlantic Ave. They always have the best buttermilk pancakes and it was close to the water. Time drifted to 11 am.

I started walking around Atlantic Ave. Looking at the beach stores. Many were closed and some were open for the fall season. I saw *Ripley's Believe It or Not* beach towels and shirts and a lot of sales during this time on beach merchandise.

The one thing that never changes have been the ocean smell, its original and the best… I walked into one of the salt water taffy stores to buy a box for my daughter. The place was called Forbes Candies, a routine I have when I'm near a taffy candy store. I wonder if the taste is different than the New Hampshire Taffy?

I walk back to the Jeep, relaxed and nervous at the same time. I've seen her entrance back to earth a few times, it took me a while to believe in this type of reality. Because I now know there are more than us on earth, the stars, the moon, the sun and this moment I'm about to see with my wife returning in a few hours. I know more is out there.

It's now about 2 pm and soon the time is about to happen. She texted me again and said "Ready?" I said, "yes, I'm ready." Her phone started making small shapes in my hand I went to the location we discussed. Time must have gone faster than I thought, it was now 2:45 pm. I started walking to the spot and as I looked around, no one was around. I put the cell in my hand and I looked at the ocean to see. I see distant water, so I keep looking, excited and just ready.

All of a sudden her phone made a noise I hear when she is arriving back, but not many humans have never heard, then the light beams of light green and yellow stream at the bottom of her phone and I looked up at the ocean to see if I can see her and from a distance I keep looking and I see two arms swimming out of nowhere. I drop everything, her phone, and mine, and I jump into the water with my clothes on and swim to her. I did not care, I just wanted to make sure she arrived home safe.

She must have reached me faster as she grabbed my hand in mid-stroke of hitting the water. We made it back to shore and she took her phone with lights and she did a full body scan with the lights and I stood there in awe, all of sudden the phone when back to normal and I sat there, wet pants and all. Hugging her I said, "You're back."

She said "Yes I'm here," and she hugged me. We started walking to the car. I think someone saw me wet with my clothes and looked at me weird, I just put both hands in the air with a joyous smile. I showed the stranger who was looking at us.

We jumped into the car I started the Jeep fast and we were going back home to the condo…She did not speak a lot but she was happy to we were back together.

I made it to the condo and my wife was looking around and she was adjusting to her surroundings again. At home and everything. I'm thinking it's like taking an airplane trip and arriving back on ground and times that by 100, I'm thinking I will never know. She keeps looking at the pictures in our condo like they were new, it took some time to really fully come back to this time zone. This why we did not talk much. I wanted her to speak when she was ready. I made sure everything was there, I had food ready for her, she seemed really hungry. She keeps looking at me to say I have a lot to tell you…I knew what she was saying without speaking and I acknowledged her by putting the palms of my hands together.

I told her to rest and I'm going to run to the office for a little bit, she nodded her head and I was out the door on my way to the *Virginia Pilot*. I could not drive with one hand, I had to use both hands from the tensions and the events of today. I arrived at the office and said hello to everyone I knew and went to Amelia's office. I knocked on the door, she was having a meeting and she held up one finger to tell me to give her a few minutes. I went back to my desk with my computer and paper, I thought and I just sat there…staring at my computer thinking about the blueprints that were given to me and all of a sudden I wanted to call Brent Brooks to catch up with him. I dialed and he picked up right away. I said "Hello."

Brent said, "Hi Marc, how are doing?"

I asked him if he bought more bizarre items. He told me "Yes and no."

I wanted to ask him about the Ocean navigational markers. When we were on the phone, we both made sure we kind of talked in code so that others wouldn't know what we were talking about. I asked him "Do you know the meaning of them?

He said, "Yes, I would go charter boat fishing many times here in the New Hampshire ocean waters." Brent went on to say out of the blue, "Ya know, Now when I worked at Lowe's there was a business account Rollins and Rollins, they bought a lot of material from us, I mean a lot. I thought it was kind of weird, I mean we had a lot of business accounts but these people would order where we had other stores to help us out to fill their order for our small ocean town."

I thought it seemed odd what Brent told me and I wrote on my notepad Rollins and Rollins. It must have been important for me to know this.

 I wanted to know more about the ocean navigational markers ...

Chapter 12

Brent went on explaining the navigational markers and what they mean. "What I saw on TV are both green and red markers in the ocean. Imagine a highway in the water, there right off the highway in the ocean and they're on the left side of the water. The green navigational markers are on the left side of the channel when entering a smaller body of water and the red for the right side while returning.

 If the waters split in another part of the water, you will see the same color markers in the water for the split of the channel waters. If you see a yellow marker there for dredging and anchorage areas plus fishnet area." I was listening to Brent with amazement on how he knew the ocean so well for ships and sailors.

"Yes", he went on, "that day I was switching channels on the TV and saw these markers in the water and I knew right away what was going on above the ocean. The ocean seemed clear. Our waters here in New Hampshire were clear waters," he said and then he asked how about the ocean there in Virginia Beach?

I went on to explain to Brent that "the waters in Virginia here have a lot of traffic. We have ports here in Norfolk, VA for cargo ships who pass in and out of the ports and there's a Navy base, it's one of the biggest bases around."

Brent said "We have less traffic here in the Northeastern waters. You know the Pacific ocean is much calmer than the Atlantic ocean."

I agreed. I had seen both ocean waters when I went to college in California, I told Brent. He went on to say he has seen both waters too. I went on to ask, "I wonder where the satellite camera was located that night you were watching on the TV."

My reporter instincts went to a thought about the Lowe's store where Brent had worked at. "Brent, do you remember you told me about a company called Rollins and Rollins, you mentioned that they purchased a lot of supplies there? Could you research more info about them there?"

Brent waited, then replied, "Sure, I can do some snooping around Lowe's".

"I tried here on Google and there's no word on the company online". I thought that was odd. I told Brent. All of sudden I hear one of his son's talk in the background on the phone and he put his hands over the phone to cover up what needed to be heard. I can faintly hear what was being said. I heard a little. He said, "Dad, when are we taking the helicopter ride over to the Wanaque Reservoir in New Jersey. This weekend still?"

He said, "Soon son, now we'll talk later okay. I'm on the phone right now Jarvis. Brent came back to the phone call, without hands blocking the sound and he said, "Marc are you still there?"

I said, "Yes I am".

"Well, listen, I will call you next week with more information about Rollins and Rollins. Talk with you soon" and the call ended.

I finished up at the office and I talked with Amelia on the way out. I said, "My wife had to go out of town for a few days and I wanted to see if all was okay."

Amelia said "Sure, I may have another story for you to report on soon since you did such a good job on the Lottery winner in New Hampshire. The owner at Landmark wants to see more stories from your desk. I smiled and moved fast to the Jeep to go home.

I was driving home and the first thing I did call my wife. She picked up the phone, but her voice sounded groggy and strong. She said, "Oh, Hi honey, how are you doing?"

I told her I was on my way home to see her and talk about things. She said, "You're not here yet?"

"I wish I could leap through the phone."

She laughed out loud at the statement for an inside joke. "I should be there soon." I was on Interstate 64 heading east and I was listening to music and thinking about my wife again.

I was thinking back to the California days and leaving college. We were packing to come to Virginia, I accepted my first job in Journalism in Hampton Roads. We were packing boxes to move and I accidentally fell on one of the boxes and hit my waist on the coffee table. I thought it broke and I needed to go to the hospital that night. I'll never forget what happened in the few minutes ahead. She said, "No you do not need a hospital." Then, all of sudden, she put her hand on my waist and I don't know what happened, it just healed; in slow motion, my waist went back in place. I didn't feel any pain as her hand was on my right side. I went into shock, thinking "Wow, I'm a lucky man" or disbelief at what just happened. I just stared at her for 10 minutes and said "Sundara, how did you do that?

She said, "Where I come from we have enhanced conditions for physical/ mental abilities and we have atmospheric adaptation, we can manipulate gravity."

My eyes opened up wide and I said in a low voice,

"In California, you can?" She said "Yes and we have regenerative healing factors as you just saw my new husband. There's more we can do, but I will stop here Honey." Then I heard in the background a honk and three times it was someone behind me at the traffic light saying to go. Again daydreaming about the past.

I look behind me and looked up and the traffic light was green. I punched my gas and my Jeep went forward fast and I put my thumbs up to the person behind me to say "Thank You" and "I'm sorry for drifting at the wheel". I drove right to our condo and pulled into the parking lot. I am walking in the door and I see two arms reach to hug me and I hug her back. "I'm home honey, I'm home" While hugging she just smiled and I knew I was at the right place at the right time.

She asked me how was work. I told her I've been calling Brent lately. He is telling me more facts, he is going to ask questions about what happened with a company there who bought a lot of material from their store when he worked at Lowe's. Sundara listened to me talk and it seemed like she wanted to tell me something.

She turned to Marc interrupting, "We need to talk honey. I have to catch you up to speed on what might be happening. You might have more weight than the Lowe's research to deal with. "

Definitely catching my attention I said, "Okay, go on."

Chapter 13

In New Hampshire, the weather had a November chill. Brent was raking the leaves at his new home by the sea. He could have hired someone to do the work but, he felt he needed the cardio and he liked the outdoors work. He had a leaf blower and couple bags and his two sons to help when they came home from school. He started working and thinking about his old jobs and Lowe's and his life before he won the lottery. He is a different person now, he can tell and its only been a month since winning the lottery, his life has changed from buying the new satellite and talking with a newspaper reporter from Virginia.

 He would have never imagined stumbling upon a channel most people have never seen. He had heard of stories of other Lottery winners; he read about a nurse who won in New Jersey $1,000 a day for the rest of her life. Many go on to support charities and local projects.

So many stories, he took some time after the leaves were raked to take a break and call his bank to make sure the accounts were set up in 5 generational gaps for the future generations of families. He was talking to his banker at Santander Bank in Seabrook. He said, "Brent you won close to $429.6 million and you know in the state of New Hampshire there is no state tax on the lottery, which is doubly good for you." Brent, he told his banker that he did not plan that to happen, winning and living here at the same time.

"I want the winnings divided into 5 installment payments for 5 generational families, meaning in the year 2020 this would be my great, great, great, and more great grandchildren."

The banker understood the arrangements that were given..."There will be more than enough for helping our family. And I want some to go to charities and the Free State Project here in New Hampshire," Brent said, and again the banker agreed, then he hung up. By the time he got off the phone both of his sons walk in, Jerry and Jarvis. They asked Dad how was he doing and he said I left you guys some leaves outside. They both looked at each other and shook their heads. Brent went on to say "our lifestyle has changed. but I want you guys to know what work is. This is going to be good for your future, there are other items I will tell you soon. The blower and the leaves are outside with lawn bags. After your homework, then the leaves."

They asked their Dad if they are still going on their trip this weekend and he told them he still has to check the reservations to make sure all is okay. They gave him the thumbs up and went to their rooms to get homework done.

As they were walking they heard their Mom call them downstairs to talk with them. They went downstairs. There she was writing a note of some sort. Margret was the organizer for the family. She said, "Make sure you guys pack for the weekend when your dad calls for the confirmation number for us to go." They both agreed and she told them "It's going to be colder in New Jersey where we are going. So pack for warmth plus we are going be in a helicopter for the trip. This is one of the nicer helicopters but still, pack for the occasion. Okay, sons?" They agreed and then she said, "Now go do your homework and the wonderful gift your Dad left you in the backyard with rakes." Both Jarvis and Jerry smirked at their Mom.

Brent was on the phone with the Sheraton Mahwah near Wanaque Reservoir. He was asking if everything is okay for their reservation this weekend. The hotel desk clerk said, "Yes everything is okay, we have two rooms rented in our top suites for weekend Mr. Brooks." Brent said "Thank you", then he went to call Flydar for the Helicopter Charter services. He said, "Mike it's me, Brent, everything okay for New Jersey?"

He replied "Yes were okay for the weekend. Did you get me a room there too in New Jersey?"

Brent had forgotten so he told Mike he would call him right back. He called and set up another room for Mike and his bodyguard, all had separate rooms. He called back and told Mike all is okay now. Mike said he would meet us at the airport as I said goodbye.

He went downstairs to talk with his wife Margret. She asked him if all was okay. He said, "Yes, all the reservation are in order for us this weekend. I had to book two more rooms for the Mike the Pilot and bodyguard.

"Nelson", she said. "O ya …So tell me more about our trip, Brent. Will we're going to a UFO Sighting that happened in 1966? Ever since you saw that channel one time you've turned into a space UFO person."

I said, "Yes I know". He went on the explain the story to Margaret. "This happened in Wanaque Reservation near the mountains, it happened on a Tuesday night at around 6:30 pm. There was a call coming into the patrol car dispatch. People were calling in saying that on the reservation they saw a huge light that looked larger than any star in the sky…He said many people drove near the gate of the reservation to see what was going on. They had to close the gate from the crowds of people. The the next day it repeated again on the water there called the "Wanaque River". I called to speak to someone there and they told me I can visit and stay on or near the reservation and walk around. I said to myself lets go…

My wife said, "Yes it would be exciting to see and visit."

Brent said he "had to stop by Lowe's before our trip this weekend, I shouldn't be that long then we leave on Friday."

She said "Okay. Make sure Nelson is with you at Lowe's, Brent. She knew her husband a new lottery winner in the state and having their bodyguard Nelson watch him at Lowe's was reassurance enough for her.

The next day Nelson and I drove to Lowe's bright and early in the morning. The parking lot brought back memories of work here. I thought to myself, this is the first time coming here since I won. It feels weird to drive and park knowing I'm not working here anymore. I have spent many years here seeing life-size posters of NASCAR Champion Jimmie Johnson #48, day after day, and helping others in the building supplies department. Nelson is walking in the door with me and I feel like a celebrity ..and when I walked through the automatic doors they treated me like one, I heard staff members say "It's Brent!"

Chapter 14

"It's Brent" waving and walking through the aisles, I thought how can I get the information needed about Rollins and Rollins…I see Richie in the painting department. He waves and asks me to stop by and I did. He said there was a man here looking for me the other day. I thought for a few seconds then I thought, "Oh that was a newspaper reporter from Virginia, he was doing a story on me and he came here to ask me questions." Now here I am doing the same for a company I thought.

Richie said, "Yes I sent him to the building supply department to talk with Jack he works now where you were working…"

"Oh really, I bet he's not better than I was."

"Well he's new Brent, and this happened all of sudden. He's been there now for a month." Then Richie shook my hand and the bodyguard watched the transaction carefully.

I walked over to the building supply area to see if there were any changes. I see Jack, I go "Hi there, I'm Brent".

He said, "Oh, I know who you are!"

I smiled and said, "Do you know where the assistant manager is?"

He said, "She's in the Appliance Department at the moment."

I said "Thank you" and I start walking. From working here a long time I instantly went to the department to meet the assistant manager. I was maybe a few feet from the area when I see legs running towards me with open arms for an instant hug and yells out loud "BRENT HOW ARE YA DOING"...Nelson stood guard and just watches and nearby.

I give her a hug and ask her could I talk with her in the back office. I had some questions to ask. She said, "Sure . . . Let's go."We start walking to the back area where a lot of our supplies and storage is located. The light is dim and others are in the back working, sorting material and boxes.

She really was excited to see, almost nervous. I know she's thinking what does he want to talk to me about. She gets her keys out to open the office and we go in. I tell Nelson it's okay you can stand nearby. Nelson said yes...I walk in and she shuts the door.

Then, over the loudspeaker, I hear "Welcome to Lowe's we running a special on Lumber today. Everyone stop by and get 10 % off of all lumber today. Only at LOWES". Then she shuts the door and it's her and me.

Talking to the assistant manager, she looked excited on what I was about to ask her. I was thinking to myself the last time she talked with me I was an employee, this time a lottery winner...I said as I sat down "Someone contacted me from Virginia to do a story."

 She said, "Yes I know, a couple of workers told me someone was in here a few weeks ago. Did you need something?"

Brent put some money on the desk and said: "Yes, I need help with some information".

 "You do not have to pay me for help Brent," as she pushed the money back to him.

 "Thank for treating me right while I worked here."

Brent went on the say "I need some information about a client here."

She says "Here? What do you need?"

Brent said, "There was a customer named Rollins and Rollins."

She said with wide eyes, "Oh yeah, I know who they are. That's a huge account here. One second let me get there file." She went to a cabinet and opened a drawer holding folders then she went on to say "They're not from Seabrook, NH. They're from a coastal area in Florida. There's a certain type of wood they want and it's only grown in New Hampshire. It is called "Squared Tree Woods." They're buying this wood from all of our Lowe's stores in New Hampshire, there shipping it somewhere but I don't know where."

"Brent." she even looked puzzled from reading their files in more in details. "This type of wood is in demand. It was already in high demand before the Rollins and Rollins started ordering the wood. But now it's really in demand. I heard this type of wood reduces wood waste and there must be another reason why they're getting this wood weekly in bulk. Brent, they buy and have it shipped to some area in Florida.

Brent asked if there was a number of them or an address in their folder. She said "Nope, we only have their name and email address. They come here with 18-wheeler trucks to get the wood and then its shipped. I wrote down the information she gave me, thinking I was doing something wrong. "Brent be careful, they seem nice but they had a coldness about them, these people…and they are one of our biggest customers". Brent understood.

She then went on to ask how my life is now and I reply "I'm the same Brent but with money and good intentions. Look I will keep in touch and thank you for helping me." Brent was very appreciated for her help. She smiled back and said, "It was nice seeing you from a different point of view." We will talk again soon thank you again".

He stood and started to walk out the door and Nelson was right outside the door. He said thank you and he walked through the store towards Nelson and his car.

While driving home from Lowe's, he thought he better call the reporter about what he learned. He went home and kept the notes in a carrying bag and started packing for the trip this weekend for the Wanaque Reservoir.

****

I was happy to talk with Sundara and catch up with her and just listen to what she had to say about her going away. I missed her a lot for being gone for three days, it was a normal leave. She goes to a place I will never go to in my lifetime. I've been to most states and overseas. I can explain these destinations in English.

There was a lot on her mind, especially what she has learned on her trip. I'm thinking about oxygen in the air, we can't see it but we know it's there and this how these next moments of understanding what my wife Sundara is going to convey to me from her trip.

We were in the same room she whispered to me. "I must write this on paper and you write back to question me back. This way we can stay in the Condo just in case someone is listening to us."

She wrote on the paper "Honey I love you first' and he wrote "I love you too. What's wrong?"

She went on to say, "I was told when I was there other people from our planet are on here on earth too!"

"There is more than just me and our daughter." I wrote down. "Really?"

She wrote "Yes", and made the head motion by nodding and mouthing yes…

I wrote "How many people?"

She said, "There are many here, they would not tell me where they're located but they're here Marc."

I wrote down "WOW." Then Marc said, "We have to find others."

Sundara replied, "Yes, we have to." She goes on to say "There are more than my kind of people here Marc!"

I took the paper and start writing, "Can you explain Honey, what you just wrote down?"

Sandura writes yes. There is a solar galaxy called Triangulum … Then Sundara took her phone out and put it in the middle of the table and tapped a button. All of sudden a holograph of three planets filled the air and I thought who did I marry at that very moment. She points with her finger and writes at the same time and said "This is Earth and this is our planet here Andromeda Galaxy and this third one, is there galaxy it's called Triangulum." Then the holograph vanished, I will show you more later honey… I stopped to think about where he saw that word before and he stood from the table to walk and was in thinking mode. I thought hard about that word and then Sandura said, "What's wrong?"

"I heard this word before" …then it came to him. I motioned to Sundara for the paper to write on.

I write and tell her about the satellite channel Brent was receiving. I ran to get my briefcase and I pulled out the envelope that said "M" on it. "It's on the plans, I saw someone drop them on my desk one day out of nowhere," I wrote. "Really?" wrote down his wife. I said "YES"… She went on to write "They are here too on your planet honey. I went home to find out more, they did not tell me everything but they told me that I'm not alone and there are others here and another kind of race is here too." I wrote, "Wow, I wonder if the Earth Surveillance Unit knows? If they knew that, why I've been followed or are they making themselves be seen? I do not know what these people know."

"There's more to tell you. Our planet is running out of hydrogen and apparently, theirs is too. So the planet Earth has plenty of unlimited hydrogen, it's easily the most abundant element in the universe but not our two planets. Now Jupiter is composed of mostly of hydrogen. Honey, it's found in the Sun and most of the stars and planets but not our two galaxies. Your planet would be fit for extracting hydrogen from seawater."

"I did not know why I was sent here. Now I know the reason, I'm here to blend in and get to know my surroundings. I didn't plan on meeting you, Marc, but I did and we both fell in love."

I wrote down "we will make it through everything that happens here... when you go home you do go home for a reason... What do we do now?"

She wrote down that "someone from my planet is supposed to find me and tell me what to do next? I have to wait. I wrote "I'm not going to wait, Sundara. We can't wait." She wrote down "We must."

I took the papers to throw them away later and safely. They both stood up quickly and hugged each other for what seemed to be forever…

Chapter 15

Brent's wife Margret likes this new lifestyle that happened a month ago because of the lottery. She has the kitchen she always wanted, and this weekend they're going to an Indian Reservation. She never thought in her lifetime that she would be talking to an Indian tribe. She was a history teacher in the local high school for many years. This moment the books become real. Jarvis and Jared were packing as well in their room, both of them had their NFL attire on. Jarvis liked the Miami Dolphins and Jarid was a fanatic about the Dallas Cowboys. It showed in their jackets and shirts. Brent had one more errand to do. That was calling Marc to update him on what was happening here from the Lowe's visit.

He took his cell phone out and shut his office door. The phone rang in the 757 area code then Marc's voice came on the phone. "Marc, it's Brent."

"Hello Brent, this is the first time you're calling me. I'm always calling you, he said.

"Yes I know, I wanted to update you on what's happened here with Lowe's."

Brent went on to say "Look I have some information from the Rollins and Rollins people at Lowe's. They're from the Florida coast and they buy wood here that is only made here in New Hampshire."

I had my notepad and asked him Brent "what type of tree you guys grow there."

Brent said it's called "Square Tree Wood, they buy in bulk here and I've learned that most of the Lowe's in New Hampshire carry this wood. It is in great demand. We have 13 stores in our state."

I just kept on writing. "I have their address and email for Rollins and Rollins. They did not have a number to reach them. The manager at Lowe's told me to be careful with them, they don't talk much at all. That's all I have on them so far, I will do more when I come back. I'm going on a family trip."

"Where you guys going?" Like a true reporter being nosy. Brent did not tell him, he said: "we're just going on a family trip for the weekend to rest and relax."

" Okay Brent," I replied. He did say much about what his wife and he talked about. "Ya know Brent if you run into that channel again call me and it doesn't matter what time of night or day, call me."

"Okay, we'll talk when I get back into town."

They both hung up and Brent went to finish packing, they were leaving early in the morning on Friday.

They brought their digital camera, smart phones, tablet, even binoculars. The whole family was excited. Brent, of course, for a UFO story and his wife for the history . . . Jarvis and Jared had both their mother's and father's genes so they both liked history and the UFO story combined.

Everyone woke up to an early to crisp October morning. Ready to go, it took them no time to arrive at the helicopter pad on Friday, this was the first time everyone rode in a helicopter. Someone suggested it when Brent worked at Lowe's, some of the rare customers who shopped there traveled this way when they went places where there was lots of traffic. For this trip, the Brooks family is taking a round-trip helicopter ride to New Jersey and flying back home to Seabrook, New Hampshire. We had an airport shuttle pick us up at the house to the tarmac at the Portsmouth International at Pease Airport in New Hampshire.

The whole family was walking, watching other planes and jets fly down the runways before going up in the air. Where the Brooks family stood there was a huge Airport hanger and in front and looking to the side they see a luxury looking Helicopter. It read on the side 'The H120'. The pilot was outside, ready for them to go aboard...the helicopter looked quite modern and fast. The Brooks' jumped in and it looked like it could seat 15 people. I'm thinking they wanted them to have room for the trip. The colors we saw on the outside looked neat, a purple and orange color.

The Brooks' twins jumped up in the air! They were all amazed at the size and looked inside the first class. Then I thought this is how the wealthy travel. The pilot said everybody please put on your helmet. There's a talking piece inside the helmet where we can all hear what's going on.

"Welcome to Charter Helicopter, we're glad you can fly with us this weekend. Everyone heard the same thing in their helmet, all four us agreed it was cool. Looks like the pilot had 1000 buttons to push, he pushed a button and the twin engines turned on. He asked if we could still hear him and we all could. The sound system was perfect even when the engines were on. My wife looked at me to give me the thumbs up.

The helmets we had on seemed to help the soundproofing inside of the Helicopter, I looked at my sons and they smiled and seem at ease. I forgot to expect motion sickness but I knew we all have been on planes together and the difference I know is the takeoff and the landing. The Pilot said, "And here we go" and the Helicopter felt like we were all in a high rise building with an elevator going up. Yes, that smooth.

All of us there, Nelson, my family and I traveling to Wanaque, NJ for a trip to the unknown. As we were traveling I had my doubts about going to see where a UFO landed many years ago but since my satellite experiences and the reporter from Virginia, I had to check it out. The pilot said those who had a window seat enjoy the view and we should be there soon.

We didn't want the trip to end soon because of the feel of the helicopter while flying it seemed like the turbulence vanished. If there was any we didn't feel this inside with our helmet. We were laughing and making sure our seatbelts were on. Then out of blue, the helicopter leaned right and we went right. You should have seen it, it was like we were doing the Zumba dance in our seats. We went with the flow of the pilot.

Jarvis and Jared remained very calm for the trip and mature for their age, looking like young new pilots in their seats. Both the boys like being in high places. You can never know what the future holds, it took about 2 hours and I see on the ground a river of water and the pilot said on the intercom system, "Welcome to Wanaque, N.J." It seemed small but big, a lot of water was surrounding the area's forest too. They were excited, it did not take that long to get here as we started to land.

On the tarmac a rental car was visible, possibly waiting for us, kind of like a modern minivan. We took our helmets off and thanked our pilot for a safe trip and he said he would catch up with us later at the hotel. We said "Okay". Nelson and all of us jumped in the van and a driver was there who took us to the Sheraton Mahwah near Wanaque Reservoir.

We noticed right away the population is smaller than Seabrook but there are more trees and water, We live in an ocean area, but here there is more river and streams and there are water towns. I noticed a lot of Native American names I saw Mohawk Ave., Minnehaha Blvd., Cayuga Ave.; the list goes on, using the names of American Indians for streets here. We pull into our hotel and it was great. I had stayed at a Sheraton before, they seem to always have good taste in the designing of a hotel…everyone had their own rooms, a total of four suites rented.

The twins had their room, Margret and I with our room, Nelson, the bodyguard and the pilot had their own separate rooms also. The hotel front desk thought we were movie stars.

At first…I told everyone I wanted to have an early start in the morning, they all agreed. We all went to our rooms and the morning arrived quickly.

We were all ready to go, we received a wake-up call from the front desk that their shuttle was waiting for us. Great service here! We jumped into the shuttle and away we went. It seemed like everything was moving fast, there was a driver in the shuttle, she said her name was Ronda Cayuga. "I will be your tour guide for this afternoon. HOW is everyone doing." I thought I remembered seeing her last name on one the roads here in Wanaque, NJ.

Her family heritage must be important here. She went on to say "Welcome to the borough in Passaic County, New Jersey in Wanaque, NJ. I will be taking you to the Reservoir to see the history of the area and the story of the UFO that was here in 1966."

Again we were all excited except for Nelson. He always has his guard up. It would not matter how others choose to be, he does his job and that's why I hired him. We were driving to the reservoir and the tour guide goes on to say, "My nationality is a Native American Indian from the Lenni Lenape. This area is called Wanaque pronounced 'Wa Na Kee', the meaning of this word means "land of sassafras".

All of us were taking in all of the information she told us and I wrote some down. We all were pretty quiet, just listening to the fascinating history being told by our tour guide.

My wife, being the History teacher thought everything she was saying is great. We go to the entrance of the Wanaque Reservoir and our tour stops talking all of sudden, to let us take in everything around us, the smells the scenery.

I wanted to know more about the Indian history here in New Jersey. She changed the subjects to the UFO facts. We stepped out of the reservoir shuttle van. All of us, Jarvis and Jared my wife and I kind of froze when she mentioned those three letters UFO, it took us by surprise why we were there. We had to let go, we all knew this is the area where a real flying object flew. We became like mannequins while she kept talking.

Chapter 16

Hannah Johnson was home waiting for her husband to return from the barracks at 5 pm. He arrives at the door at 5:20 pm. Right on time, she knows when her hubby's coming in from duty at the base. He kisses her on the cheek and said, "Hi April," a nickname he gave his wife."Hi, how was work on the base today?"

He said, "We have to talk honey."

She said, "Go ahead, I'm ready."

Harold sat down, put both hands on the kitchen table and told Hannah, "I can't explain everything honey. I can say this. We're moving our whole family again.

Hannah looked into the air and she put both hands on the table with Harold and asked, "Where are we moving to?"

Harold said "It was not like any base we have ever been on. It's really a futuristic mission, honey. They chose me for training for one year. I have never seen or heard of this type base in my life."

His wife said "Really".

"Yes...and I need your support more than you know."

Hannah called the children into the living room and she told them "Guess what guys, we're moving!" They both looked puzzled. Zelda and Nolan were a bit emotional and you could feel it in the air. They wanted to say not again, another move, this has happened to them 3 times already and it is a part of their life, the unexpected move.

Zelda and Nolan knew not to get too close to others because we will have to detach from other people when we have to move again.

"It's not easy for us but we like the adventure of moving to a new place with a fresh sense of scenery and personalities. The military lifestyle and home life, they are two separate things," Harold thought to himself while explaining the move.

"Yes, we have to move again, everyone."

Nolan asked, "Where Dad, where?"

Harold told the kids, "I do not know yet. It's going happen within a month, I know we must get ready and pack and make sure our family housing is clean. We all know the routine." All four agreed to the words being said.

That was hard for Harold to explain to his family that they had to move again. He told himself this was for the good of his family and country. And he signed up for the military for both causes and he did his best at both. He went to sleep wondering where they will be stationed. He figured he will find out in the morning.

The trumpet sounded at 5:30 am on base and he woke up. The daily routine begins again, he switched on the news while putting on his fatigues and Army boots, which were always cleaned and polished. He kisses his wife, opened the doors to his children's rooms to see if they were safe and he heads to the barracks.

He passes by a few tanks and a statue of General Custer on a horse and he was thinking about his future the whole time. He jumps out of his car and walks towards the building where his handprints are his ID now…Soldiers saluted as he walked by and he sees a security scan. One of the soldiers says "They've been expecting you 2nd Lt. Johnson." The soldier saluted and Harold saluted back.

He put his handprints on the elevator and went inside. The elevator door opened and Harold went over to the room where he was to meet the Colonel. The Colonel was waiting in the room. He stands up, Harold saluted him first and Colonel Mathews returns the salute and says, "At ease Johnson. How is everything going?"2nd Lt. Johnson said, "I don't know what to say, excited about what's happening and don't know the unknown side of the mission."

The Colonel said "We know. We have to take you and your family to a secret base … this is a place not many people know about, and all three infantry units are hidden from the public eye… We ask that you pack your items with a moving truck that we provide for you. We have hired someone to drive your moving truck there and all members of the family will be flown to the destination. We can't mention where until we are up in the air, traveling to the base including yourself ." The 2nd Lt. looked surprised but he knew this was not going be your everyday Army move.

"We're asking if you can be ready 30 days from today, okay?""I will make sure," the 2nd Lt. stated.

The Colonel went on to say if you need time we can give you more time."

"All three units have followed the same protocol. I will be checking in from time to at this location for questions and updates. You were picked for this unit because of your leadership skills and extraordinary thinking process. And I do mean this, many did not make it this far 2nd Lt. Harold Johnson. We choose all backgrounds for this mission and various ranks as well. Yes, you're an African American Army Officer. Just remember the military standards. The Colonel went on to express a metaphor.

"2nd LT Harold Johnson let me ask you something, have you ever had a good Garden Salad?"2nd Lt. Johnson said, "Yes I've had many. The Colonel goes to explain "There are many ingredients to this great monstrosity with a combination of tomatoes, olives, onions, and croutons while adding fresh lettuce." The Colonel raised his voice and said:

"This explains the Military.! Period."

The 2nd Lt. got it right away and replies, "Sir, Yes Sir!"

I'm honored to be in the Army, Colonel Mathews. We will be ready in a month's time."

"Please call us and a moving truck will be there at your home and I wanted to explain your pay rate for the new infantry will increase more than I can say at the moment." Colonel Mathews stood up and I did too, he saluted Harold and he returned a salute with distinguished manners. "Thank you, Colonel."

As Harold was walking out, someone leaving before him gave him a sealed folder and Harold decided to wait until he got home to open it. He was driving home, thinking about his family and how they have been with him on all of the moves and to stay in one place would be new for us. It seemed to fit our personalities to see other cultures and meet new people.

The Johnson family, in the last six years, have been to Georgia, Alaska, and Germany and now to an undisclosed base many have not heard of. The pages in the chapter keep turning.

As he was driving home to see his wife Hannah and children, he glanced at the folder that was handed to him, wondering what was in the paperwork. Maybe they mention where we are going to be stationed?Harold hugged his wife as he walked through the door and she asked him right away if they told him where they were going. He said "Nope, they didn't tell me yet. The unit where I'm being stationed is very secretive. At this point, we will not know till we're there. We have to pack and they will move our items there, April."

"Really Harold?"

"This is the all I can say. And they gave me a folder to read. How have Zelda and Nolan been today?"His wife said, "They were doing well, they did their homework and are excited about moving, but also little worried. ".

"Yes, I know this move is a little different Hannah."

"Open the folder, let's see what it says."Harold opened the seal on the folder and there was only one piece of paper. It said to '2nd Lt. Johnson and Family, The Welcome Package for Operation Space Sahara2O'. He thought what a name for an operation! There are two military logos on both sides of the top of the page he did not recognize. Only the subject line was filled out at the top: "Space Marine Infantry Unit 1/3."

Basically, It was an instrution folder. The next line said"Packing for the Unit"Hello 2nd Lt Johnson family. We want you to pack everything you would normally pack . Harold kept reading then he did a double take...He kept reading.This training facilitties will not allow plastic in bold letters the phrase reads

" NO PLASTIC "

All plastic has to be removed. He wondered why they could'nt bring plastic with them. Most of everything they own has plastic, from there phones to computer monitors. How is he going to tell his children that they can't bring plastic with them ? He would have to explain, even for him it's going to be extremely difficult. The letter goes on to state, When there packing is completed, a moving truck will help load up all housing material. Please call the three digital numbers, It said # 832. When your ready.

The next subject line stated travel arrangements will be done by train and airplane and the moving company will give you the tickets and instructions. Harold looked at his wife and she looks back at him. Harold just handed her the piece of paper because if he told her what the paper said she would not believe him.Hannah said "Harold, this is a big mission you have been asked to go on. No Plastic at all? Not Tupperware or blue ray machines?"

Harold said "nope"

Then she said, "What are things made of where we're going then? You ever ask yourself that Harold?"

And again he said "No I did not until now …

****

I was happy when I received the information about Rollins and Rollins from Brent. He is being really cool with me. I hoped I would be that cool if I won that much money in a Lottery. I thought about it, yes, the answer is yes. I would be this cool if I won that much money with my wife and daughter.

I was going over everything we talked about on paper. I gathered my notes on the desk to piece them together and try to figure out what it all means. I'm a newspaper reporter, I've been trained to put together bits and pieces of news to find the real meaning. Somehow, though, my mind was not connecting the pieces.

I get a text from Amelia. "Where have you been lately, Mr. Reporter from the Beach?"

I texted her back. I told her "I was with my wife, she's back from being out of town for awhile. I was coming into the office this afternoon to talk."

Amelia texted back "Okay, I'll see this afternoon." I was looking over the desk of notes from the surveillance earth unit, the notes from Brent, the Rollins and Rollins information and notes from my wife's trip, just trying to figure out what's happening and I came to a conclusion. I started to think backward from meeting my wife to meeting Brent Brooks. Then I thought there must be something on our planet that someone wants badly. Something with hydrogen and the ocean water or just water? Something that their planet does not have. Supposedly, I do not know what it is or how many people or beings are involved or why...

This what I'm seeing on my notes so far. Then I thought where to go next with this theory...

Maybe my wife knows why. She didn't tell me everything and there's a lot more to explain to me. I decided to send an email to Rollins and Rollins first from the email address Brent gave me. My wife was out running errands and my daughter was in school.

 How would I write the email? Okay, I know what I can do. I wrote the email telling them I was visiting New Hampshire and trying to find Square Tree Wood, would they know where to find some? In the subject line of the email, I wrote: "In Search of." I will wait for a response. While I was staring at the computer screen, I felt it was time to leave the condo, get some fresh air, smell the Atlantic waters, and find shells on the shore. This was one of the perks you receive from living near the ocean.There were many thoughts and facts floating in the air and having a change of scenery could help me. While I was there I asked a stranger questions for my case. A lot of times asking others who live near the water, "Water People" as I called them, they know more than what people think.

I've always thought just like the ocean, those who live near the ocean remind me of low tides to high tides. You never know how ocean water will be daily, it's flexible, rough, and mellow. You have to pay attention to see.

As I was driving on Atlantic Ave. on the oceanfront, I noticed two trucks behind me, kind of like when I was followed in New Hampshire. I keep driving the speed limit and then I look back in the rearview mirror and they were gone. Then as soon as I stopped at a traffic light, my phone rings and it's Sundara. She sounded frantic on the phone. "Honey are you there?"

"Yes, I'm here."

Chapter 17

She says, "There were two black pickup trucks parked at the house just sitting. I couldn't see in their windows, they were tinted."

"They were just following me here on the beach right now."

"Do you want me to call the police now."

"No, not yet. Don't worry. If you don't hear from me within a ½ then call the police to the oceanfront. Deal?"

"Deal. Be careful, they were here at the house waiting outside for about 5 to 7 minutes."

"Okay, love you, my wife."

"Love."

I kept glancing behind me in the mirror. No one there, I think they're gone. I make a right on 56 Street. Then all of a sudden one of the black trucks that was following jack hammered me so I could not move, one in front me and one of them was behind me. I went to call 911 on my phone and my phone cut off, like the life on my phone vanished and my engine turned off by itself . . . then my automatic windows went down by themselves. Next to me, all of a sudden there was one person in the passenger's seat of my Jeep and the other in my back seat and voice spoke that was human, but then again it sounded not human.

"Hello, Dazet. We would like to speak with you for few moments." My heart was pumping 1000 miles a minute. "I be quick," he said. "We been watching you for a couple weeks, would like to ask you questions?" I did not see a face, I just saw dark purple outfits, each wearing a baseball hat.

I went on to say, "I do not know what you're talking about and how did you get into my truck?" I thought to myself, my wife should be sending the cavalry soon to the beach to find me.

The objects said, "Did you get our envelope on your desk that said "M? We were watching in New Hampshire. You only see us because we want you to see, otherwise, you would never know we here."

I thought 'let me take a deep breath and listen for a change instead of asking all the questions as a reporter.'

"Dazet, there's been some events that have taken place around the water, that become quite a concern to us…Would you know anything about this?"

I said "no"; I had to lie. I did not know what they would do with me.

"Those plans we sent you are from one of the members involved with water… We work for the surveillance unit. Dazet, we know more than you think…"

I thought what do they know?

"We want you to keep pursuing your hunches. We will be nearby wherever you go. Believe it or not, we're on your side …Keep following hunches!" One of our associates talked with on the phone at your offices .

All of sudden three Virginia Beach Police sirens grows closer to the two trucks. I look out the driver's side of the window, maybe for half a second and I turn around and there was no one, the two trucks were gone like it never happened. Then my car turned back on and my phone was back like it never turned off and the police were in front my car.I felt like was it a dream or was it real? The police were here asking if I was safe…police lights everywhere.

I said, "Yes I'm fine."The police went on to say they got a call on 911, "Your wife called in and told us you were being followed, we got here as fast as we could."I told them I'm okay and what happened was kind of a blur.

"Thank you for getting here when you did officer."

The officer asks if I wanted to file a report and I said nope I was fine. The police officers went to their cars and said if there is any more trouble do not hesitate to call. When they left I kept my composure until they were gone. My hands on the steering wheel started shaking. My wife called me and said, "Are you alright …OMG, are you okay."

"Yes, I'm fine and thanks for calling the police. What a day I've had today. How's Laura? Are you safe over there?"

"Yes."

"I was worried about you honey…I'm on the way home now. My nerves are already shot. I will be driving the speed limit tonight."

"Take your time husband, just get home safe," my wife said.

I received a text from Brent, "Hi Marc, it's me texting you from New Jersey." I told myself that's where they're vacationing. He did say he was going to be gone for the weekend.

I told him "I'm fine," but my nerves were still in overdrive. He said they were visiting a Reservoir in the area.

 "The tour guide here was about to tell us more information, I will talk soon." I texted back "Okay Brent, talk soon."

****

We all gave our attention to Rhonda Cayuga, our tour guide, as she explained her family history to them in New Jersey. She said, "I am from a large family broken up into many parts."

Margaret, being a history teacher, wanted to showcase her knowledge of the American Indians. Then all of sudden Jarvis and Jared took over the tour by saying, "Okay tell us about the UFO sightings, Ms. Tour Guide." She laughed and shook her head and then became real serious.

She said, "Okay I will tell you as we are walking the reservoir, then I will tell about our Indian culture here in this part of the New Jersey." They all became quiet including Harold, this was one of the main reasons he came here...to find out if the story here relates to his newfound TV channel and possibly help Marc with his story.

Our tour guide goes on to say, "It happened in 1966. Many of the eyewitnesses saw this happen here. It was not in the news a lot about what happened. Even today you will not know much about it…It was cold in September here and over here," she pointed to the water and resources on the reservoir, "this is where the mass sighting happened."

"The UFO appeared to be hovering over the Wanaque Dam and our water resource facilities, there was a lot of snow and ice over the water area. Then, what seemed to be white light and multiple color beams flashed down to make holes in the ice…where our water is located here."Brent looked at my wife as Rhonda was explaining what happened here and he immediately went to the word water again from the channel he saw with the navigational markers…

Rhonda continued "Many people witnessed this event happening from start to finish. That night did go on record that it happened. Words like terrified, goose bumps, and 'I've never seen anything like that in my entire life' were some of the witness statements" … Jarvis and Jared's eyes got wider as she keeps on explaining.

"Pictures were taken that night from other people who were witness to the event, the police received many phone calls about what happened. After the event happened, there where women and men dressed in dark purple who appeared throughout our town, they seemed like they worked for a higher unit organization, not sure or UFO investigators, they were all over the place asking questions…"

A pin could drop on the ground and no one would not have heard it. The Brooks' ears were glued to our tour guide.

"What's odd is on the very same date and time in another town, the same sighting happened in Myerstown, Pennsylvania Reservoir, and their water resources"…All of them gasp again …

The location in Pennsylvania is about 200 miles from here… Brent thought "Wow, I have to take a picture of this historical UFO site and send it to Marc in Virginia." Brent snapped the picture of the sign and words and tapped his phone and the picture was gone to Virginia.

****

I heard a beep on my phone and opened the text. I wondered what I was looking at; it was a picture and it said UFO Sighting at Wanaque Reservoir, New Jersey. I stared at the picture and was puzzled a little, then another text came in to say "Marc, this a true story. It happened in 1966. They mentioned there we people here dressed in purple right after it happened. I think UFO investigators came here to ask the community questions about what happened."

I wonder if they where the Surveillance Earth Units back then. The two people I spoke to who cornered me here in the truck at the oceanfront wore purple too.

Strange that event happened in 1966 and it's 2017 now…Brent kept texting. "The tour guide told us beams of light put holes in the ice where water was located here on the reservoir and it happened at another location near water at a Pennsylvania Reservoir…"

I knew that this was not a coincidence again, hearing the word "water" again… I paused for a moment to gather my thoughts and then I texted Brent back."Can you ask the tour guide there what month did this happen in?"

There was a pause then a text came back. "It happened in September and October in 1966".

"Okay Brent, thank you. Talk with you soon. The reporter from Virginia!"

****

Brent noticed the tour guide walked closer to his family and leaned in to ask, "I would like to invite your family to a Lenni Lenape Indian dinner".Brent looked at my wife and the twins, they all agreed "yes" at the same time. "Yes, we would like to, when and where?"

"I will pick you up at the Sheraton at 7:00 pm to come over and see our culture."

They all agreed and were already excited about the dinner.

Chapter 18

They arrived back at the hotel early from a day they did not expect. Brent took a lot of pictures and took notes. His family was excited about having dinner with the people from this area and to learn more about the Native American Indian culture; this would be a first for us. Margaret kept saying that was really nice of Rhonda to do this for our family.

Seven pm came quickly at the hotel and the Brooks' family were ready to go. Then all sudden a luxury van pulled in. They watched to see who it was for as the automatic windows rolled down. It was Rhonda, the tour guide. "Hey, come on, jump in," she said. Nelson joined them but their pilot stayed back, he was having fun just relaxing in the room without going anywhere in the air …day in and day out.They all jumped in the van and away they went. She said, "I hope you're hungry and have an open mind on what you're about to see and hear.

"They all said "Yes" and Jarvis said, "After hearing about UFO's today our thoughts are open and hungry." Both twins high-five each other as the van door shut. Margaret smiled at Brent to show how happy she is on this trip and she threw him the thumbs up sign. Harold did the same.

The rural parts of New Jersey came to life until they came to a sign out of the blue that said: "Welcome To The Lenni Lenape Native American Home." The sign was colorful and had animals on it – a wolf, turkey, turtle, and a design of feathers. Brent had never seen a sign like this in his life.

Their tour guide asked, "How did you like the tour today of the reservoirs?" They all agreed it was the best and alarming too. She went on to ask, "What do you know about the Native American Indian?"Margaret said she knew a lot from being a history teacher. They drove past the sign and saw many single level buildings. Then they came to a building where people outside were waiting for them with gifts and shoes and a kind heart. It was really nice for Rhonda Cayuga to invite them to experience her culture. They entered a building and there were more people there.

 It was unreal, they brought them to a room, Brent saw a long table with chairs and on the table were clams, oysters, and scallops on one side of the table. Then what seemed to be wild plants, nuts, berries, fruits, there was pizza there too. Brent was surprised to see this on the table. They saw steak . . . There was a lot of food.The family sat down and noticed there were food dishes I didn't recognize. Their tour guide told them what each item was. She pointed and said this is called Salpon (Frybread) and over here this is Shewahspan (Grape Dumplings). They were eager to try them all. The tour guide told them that they observe Thanksgiving for 10 to 12 days.

"It's called 'Gamwig'. You see, our tribe is scattered throughout the state of New Jersey, so when we come together for any event it's a happy moment to meet each other and eat."

"Our tribe takes from the waters, land, and forest and only take just enough needed." We sat down and they made them feel like they were tribe members, very nice the people here. They told them there were about 16,000 Lenape now living in four states, ranging from New Jersey to Pennsylvania. They all started eating and sharing stories, it was a great time – the trip as a whole.

****

Meanwhile Back in Virginia . . .

When I got home I googled more information about what happened in New Jersey and the UFO sightings. Sundara came into the room with the phone and said, "Honey, look at my cell phone." It started making a beacon noise and glowing. It was not the same when my wife vanished into the water, it had a different color and new noise.

Sundara suddenly said, "Someone is trying to Emllger to me…"

"What, really?"

 She said "Yes you see my phone, how it's acting. They're trying to connect with me here on earth!"

"What should we do Sundara?"

"They will find me in person. This is our tradition, we just have to wait."

All of sudden we get a knock on our door. It startled Laura, she came out of her room asking is everything okay. I went to the door to open it and as I opened it there was no one there. I peeked around the corner, looked down both sides and there was no one there…I shut the door and said, "Sundara, there is no one there."

She did not respond and I called her name again, no answer. I looked around the corner and there was a note saying she'd be right back and she was gone that quick. She left and I thought to myself "what just happened? How did she leave that quick?"

Laura was sitting there looking at me, frightened to say what she saw and I didn't . . . she looked to me, "Is she coming back Dad?"

I thought, I never saw this happen before, all the years we have been together…"Whoa, where did my wife go, where did she go?" I opened the door to look down the hallways again to see any signs of her nearby…

All of sudden the hallways seemed to change. It became increasingly colder and I noticed right away, she was here. She must have done that on purpose to show she was here.

Sundara noticed she was somewhere underwater. She looked around and there was a person who was walking towards her. The lady spoke, she said "Aradnus" and spoke a language she could only understand. She said a name again, "Aradnus", she came through to answer and understand this was her true name. She spelled it backwards for protection and she thought the same with her daughter name's Laura, true name being Arual.

She said it again, "Aradnus." This time much louder and her response back as she came through, she said to herself "where am I?".

The lady told her "you're at an Ooynt Extraction location here on earth" …
Aradnus knew the plans being done and this was the first time she got to see
this in action, she worried she would never make it back to her child and
husband at the condo.

Aradnus was taken to a room where others were standing. It seemed like they
were waiting for her arrival before having a meeting with about 20 people
there…The temperature in the room adjusted from cold to warm to hot
simultaneously …and no one aged a day.

"From our planet of Oynt we can control our aging from younger toddler…
meaning some of us in this room are 100 or more years old and some are
younger in thought. Once we reach a certain age we can go forward or
backward in age if we choose…We notice we can observe a lot within our race
and others...We have not met many who can stop aging from happening…," the
woman explained to Sundara.

The lady guided her to sit down. There was a seat there with the name Aradnus
and she sat in the chair and it felt like a perfect fit, it was more than a chair. It
seemed like a living chair, it had devices to touch and the seat fits all
personalities. This chair can retrieve your history and others Sandura sat down
and quietly asked how her husband and daughter were doing and the chair was
way more advanced than Google. It showed video of them safe and sound while
worrying where I was at…They were safe and Sundara was happy. Then all of
the people in that room became quiet because someone was going to speak.

"Hi Aradnus, Welcome back."

They spoke in her language dialect but she chose English to translate it to show to them I want to go back home...to my husband and daughter. She was the only one.

They kept on with the talks. "We are bringing you here to show you in person one of the many areas where we are extracting ocean waters to make hydrogen. We have studied the process for many years and we are just showing you now..."

"The reason we have you here is there is another race from the Triangulum Galaxy which is not too far from our galaxy who are in search of seawater as well and other material here. We heard there is a movement of them on earth. This race has their talents too but they're not willing to share.

Our race is scattered all over the earth. Their galaxy is very new to living on earth and harsh. We're peaceful people but if we have to be aggressive we can be this way. War with them and the humans would not be in our better interest. Those from the Triangulim Galaxy have different skills than us and again can be nice and then mean in a half of a second. We're going to give you something, it's an item that will let us have the same skills from the Triangulum Galaxy. We do not want you to learn their skills, it will just happen when you need it and you use it. This is only for you and only you to have …

There are three races, you have access to two, you know ours well and the humans and now the Fiwusho of Triangulum…Sundara asked "Why do you want me to have this access compared to others of us on earth? Why me?

"Well you now have access to a lot of money on earth through your earth husband's friend…and you have connected yourself with a mate who is a reporter and can find information about all that's happening and they're getting close to a lot of information. We see from here you will have to be careful Aradnus, you will have the 3 energies in time. We will call on you to add more but right now, three races are fine."

"There is a lot going on and again, if we have to have a war we will, but we do not want a war with humans or Fiwusho. By the way, as the translation went through the Fiwusho have pets, the same as humans. I see humans have dogs, cats, and rabbits plus much more. The Fiwusho have their own pets too, not to alarm you but they have them too…"

"We will talk again soon."

The people at the table of 25 agreed. The next thing Sandura knew was she felt light-headed and just fell asleep and she could hear the girl who brought her there saying, "I'm going to bring you back to the hallway safely and we will talk more in the future." Next thing she knows she is back at the condo hallway in Virginia Beach, wondering what just happened.

She just sat there, frozen, and yelled out "Marcccc". The door from their condo flew open and she sees Marc leap outside of the condo in a rush. He was yelling "Sandura, oh my god, where have you been, where have you been?"

She said "Back, I had to go without notice. Let's go inside and I'll explain more."Marc picked her up so she could stand and she barely walked in the door on her own. She was tired and had an interesting smile on her lips like she knew something I would never understand.

Sundura went straight to sleep. We all calmed down from what seemed like a panic moment for a couple hours. I was watching her rest and I started to daydream again about the moment I wanted to marry her.

It was right after we were in the commitment ceremony in California and everyone had the cap and gown on outside in the warm air. We were young and ready to go out into the world. We were listening to the commencement speaker, Shirley Sandberg, I remember like it was yesterday.

She said "When the challenges come, I hope you remember that anchored deep within you is the ability to learn and grow. You are not born with a fixed amount of resilience. Like a muscle, you can build it up, draw on it when you need it. In that process, you will figure out who you really are - and you just might become the very best version of yourself." At the

end of the speech, there outside with a crowd of thousands, the outdoor air suddenly turned quite cold and everyone looked around to see how that happened. The air went from warm to cold in a half a second people were shivering and I knew that instant I wanted to marry that girl and she wanted to marry me. I looked at where she was sitting and she looked back at me. Then the air went back to warm, even the speaker who spoke the quotelooked puzzle from what happened ...everyone went on with the ceremony like nothing happened but not me, I knew.

Chapter 19

Harold look around as Hannah read the Military Memo given to her. She said "No plastic on this move. really? Do you have the phone number to the commanding officer who issued this memo, Harold?"

I said "No, I didn't like the idea either. We can do it. There hasn't been any challenge we have not met face to face."

Hannah's response was "This is a Mega roller coaster going backward type of challenge honey!"

"I know it. I will tell the Zelda and Nolan, they will not be happy about this. You need to take them to the movies and whatever they ask for within reason they should get."

"You're right." Hannah went back to tell the children about the memo and I see both of them look at me to say, "No Way Dad".

"I know, look I'll make it up to you between now and the move, you can choose what you want – movies, ice cream, and shopping spree, no plastic, though."Nolan said "I wonder what we can buy that has no plastic in it" and both the brother and sister looked at each other and said, "Where are we going?"

Weeks went by, the Johnson's started packing for this new chapter. They had fun and were mad at the same time. They had to let go of a lot of things there, the board game they kept them except substituted the plastic pieces with metal game board pieces from other games. There was a checklist each one of them had to make sure the move went smoothly as could be. Some heartache occurred over letting go of some items but they knew in order to go forward it must be done. A half month went by and a phone call came in from Colonel Mathews asking if all was okay for the move. 2nd Lt Harold Johnson told the Colonel that all was okay and they would be ready in week;

The next day in the mail there was a manila envelope addressed to our family. I opened it and there was a total of what seemed to be eight tickets, four train tickets and four airplane tickets for the trip. There were multiple color Travelers Checks inside also and then something odd, it looked like another type of currency. I never saw anything like this before, there was a lot of it in the envelopes. They were numbered 1,3, 5,7,...23... on up to 103, all odd numbers on the currency for some reason. He took it and put it away to keep the travelers check nearby.

I kept saying to myself "where are we going?" I was excited but also quite protective of my family, Things were going to get quite interesting. We were almost ready and I had the idea to take the family the newest "Star Trek" movie released. It was playing at a theater nearby in Junction City, Kansas near the base. They enjoyed every minute of it. I grew up with Captain James T. Kirk and the Starship Enterprise for a long time and the whole family are still fans today in Kansas.

I was sitting in the theater next to Hannah. Many would not know my wife was from the island of the Commonwealth of the Bahamas. The capital city is Nassau, the small island population is 22 thousand people. Many people go on vacation there from all cultures and the natives are tough, adventurous people. You're asking why, well because before any hurricane comes to the United States most will travel to Caribbean waters first before going on to the shores of the states .. And this why they're a very tough people with hospitality all in one.

We came home from the movies to relax and the next day I received another phone from Colonel Mathews. He wanted to know if we were ready for the move and said a moving company would be coming there on Monday and on Wednesday we will make sure you're on the train near the base in Topeka. "Did you receive all the tickets by mail?"

I answered "Yes I did…Okay then, Wednesday it is." The time seemed to stop after that call for our family. It was like a countdown for New Year's Eve. Then it happened, Monday out of nowhere an 18-wheeler Atlas Moving truck pulled up in front of our house. The truck doors opened and it looked like a NASCAR pit crew came out to change tires etc... Five moving guys shot out of the truck. They said, "Hello sir, we here to help you move."

I said, "Yes, okay great." I knew by saying yes it meant that, to quote Dorothy from the Wizard Of Oz, "We won't be in Kansas anymore" …

The moving crew moved like lighting taking our boxes, scanning them. They had a tool that scanned each box. I asked them what they were doing and they said it checking for plastic, to make sure the boxes are okay for the move.

It was a tool I have never seen in my life. All four of us stood watching as the five men were moving our items with a supreme quickness.

Other people called to wish us the best and they expressed how they're going miss us…it took about five hours, the truck was packed. Some of the boxes we had to repack to make sure their scanners equaled an okay.

My wife and I and the children looked around at an empty house …They were done and we were amazed, we had many moving trucks from our other moves but this one was different.

The person in charge said all of your items will be there safely when you arrive as planned…he shook my hand and I said "Okay".

Looking around the house, you could hear echoes between the rooms as we spoke.

Hannah asked, "Tomorrow, what time are they picking us up for the train part of the trip?"

"The Colonel said around 3 pm."

"Let's go get some Dairy Queen and grab some sundaes, honey before we go tomorrow."

We drove slowly off the base looking at the statue of General Custer on the base. And we ate our sundaes slowly and we were excited too. Zelda asked me, "Dad, do you think we will have Dairy Queen where we are going?"

I told her "they better if they want to keep our family there…"

On Wednesday as planned, a car was waiting in our driveway. It looked like a modern Hummer, the windows tinted and I was thinking they're here. We were peeking out the window looking at the cool-looking wheels and shape of the Hummer. I looked around the house to see if there were any last minute items I left behind. Everything was clear. jumped in there was soldier dress in the uniform I saw at the barracks the in the newer fatigue colors.

The soldier came out of the car and saluted me and I did the same. This soldier was in the modern uniform I saw at the barracks. They were different from the old uniform, newer fatigue colors. He was wearing some sunglasses too. The soldier opened the door for my family to jump on in. We jumped in and drove to Topeka, Kansas for the Amtrak. Just like that, we were at the main gate of the base that said: "Welcome to Fort Riley, Kansas."

Chapter 20

Margret was very happy having a dinner with Native American Indians, a first in her life. She taught about this in her class and here she is in the truest form, having food from many traditions. The twins were happy too and I felt like I had been adopted by the Lenni Lenape Native American people. I was having fun and in tune with what was happening. One native person there asked our tour guide in their language a question. And the tour guide paused then

she said in English, "Do you know the story of the Native American Indians in the US?"

My wife knew and you could tell she wanted to say something but she did not. The man started talking and our tour guide translated to us in English and it seems like he had a lot to say. Rhonda translated for him, he said that "in 1850 all native American Indians Tribes, about 360,000 at the time, lived west of the Mississippi River, some from the Northwestern and Southwestern areas. This was considered the Indian Territories now in the present day Oklahoma while the Kiowa and Comanche shared land in the southern plains."

We were still eating and even Nelson, our bodyguard, stopped chewing his food just to hear every word that was said at that table. We were all in awe at what was being said. He kept talking as Rhonda translated and we kept our ears open. Rhonda further translated, "the Sioux, Crows, and the Blackfeet lived in the northern plains. The native American encountered adversity from the steady flow of European immigrants into northwestern cities. There was a push of immigrants into the western lands, which was already occupied by a variety of Native American Tribes."

The elder member who was talking, his hands were like an invisible map explaining the area of the states and we all understood. Again Rhonda continued for the elder, "He said he would keep it short, his talks, the US gained control of the borders to expand land to what is now Texas, Oregon, and California with Arizona.

My wife seemed to know as she shook her head in agreement on what was being said. I was thinking abut what was said and the UFO sighting in the past that happened here. He went on to say that "more people started coming into the US," talking with his hands again, went wide to describe the US like he was saying "WOW" with his hands, "many went west for "Gold" . . .

"When America started to become an independent nation," he kept on talking and we were still intrigued and we started eating again as he continued sharing, "Many began to make the western area their homes. There were policies made between the Native American Tribes and the US. To put this, in short, the goal for the US at the time was for us to adopt and become citizens like others with laws and policies ..."

He said "there were stories that we harm others who weren't native American but that was far from the truth. We helped many settlers adjust to their new surroundings by selling food and in fact played a role in sending messages between wagon trains to help others to settle in. But many were in fear that they were still going to be attacked by tribes even though we were nice."

Again he keeps talking and we were eating and it seems like we were at a campsite outdoors while he told us more of the story. Jarvis asked how have many tribes survived today? Rhonda asked the elder the question. "They tried to break up our culture with Indian Schools to adapt to the US customs and ways. In time, he said, in 1887 there was a treaty called The Native American Treaties with the United States." I thought to myself when we were in school we were taught differently, some parts were obviously left out and here we get to know the truth.

My wife did not start eating yet, she was glued on what was being said. I wondered if the UFO sighting had anything to do with the Native American Indians…He said the policy stated at the time that the lands that were -occupied then basically made the Native Americans wards of the U.S.

"The US wanted ownership of the land by separating it into reservations which were owed and given to each family to have a plot of land." He said to our translator "the rest of the land was sold to the settlers. The Treaty stated that each family was given the option to have between 80 to 120 acres of land…"

That's when my wife said "Really?" I was stunned by her saying this, I was learning too, we all were…He said "unmarried persons received between 40 to 60 acres of land. This worked out for a little while but with American laws, many of our traditions were taken away and the many Native American lost their lands to be resold to settlers moving in…"

"In order to survive, they forced Native Americans to sell their lands and this made a divide because a lot of the land that was sold to others or destroyed were lands of spiritual and cultural concern to our tribes." The elder member talking pointed to himself….and we all just stared into space imagining what he was saying and how they must have felt back then. He said "a lot of people did not make it and our population grew smaller he went on to say…He said "I have one more thing to say" and we thought our brains could not hold more that was said today. He said to Rhonda, "our tribe here in the Northeast is a huge tribe, we are divided into many groups and sub-groups. One is the "WOLF". He said, "Took-Seat, they have 12 sub groups under the Wolf

section of our tribe." He made the hand description of a Wolf and we got it when she said it…"Next section of our Tribe is called The "TURTLE" Poke-koo-un'go," he said. "They too have many sub-groups the number is 12.

"Subgroups for Turtle would be Snapping Turtle Lee-kwin-a-I, Little Turtle We-lung-ung-sil. Then we have a Third Group called the "TURKEY"Pul-la'-ook, they too have 12 subgroups. Like the Scratch the Path Moo-har-mo-wi-kar'-nu or the Pine Region Koo-wä-ho'ke."

"Our customs are still here today." All of us looked at each other and I started doing the math, they have 36 different sub-tribes within the main three tribes. Whoa, I thought…I'm sure there are more main groups not mentioned here today…he just mentioned three…We enjoyed the history and sharing of their culture. It was a once in a lifetime experience to be here.

Chapter 21

The Hummer was really modern for the trip to the train station. I didn't know they made them this modern I said to his wife Hannah. The children were in the back as everyone was excited about the next step. The Amtrak station was not too far from the base …When they arrived the driver seemed like he went to a back road, a private road entrance. The automatic gates opened near the train's main office.

And there was our train, it did not look like an Amtrak train at all. There wasn't a logo on the side. There were soldiers there to greet us and we jumped out of the Hummer, thinking to ourselves "where are we going?"

We all jumped on the train: Zelda, Nolan, my wife and I and as I was looking around I noticed on this train there was no one but us was on it and the car must have been eight cars wide.

It was just us. My son, being the curious type, wanted to see the rest of the train. He started walking down the aisles into the next car, nobody there and the next one no one, it went down five cars into the dining car and he sprinted back to our train's caboose and said almost yelling "LOOK AT THE DINNING CAR THEY HAVE FOR US"…I told him to sit down but he

didn't, he waved to his sister Zelda to come let me show you! She jumped up and went with Nolan to check out the train that offered food. She had the same reaction as Nolan, "What? Now that's a lot of food and drinks. They have everything on here, a lot breads of all types, there's raisin bread, whole wheat. The sign there for Indian bread and many types sitting there. All types of fruits, apples, tangerines, mangoes.

It looked like they went to great lengths to make sure everything was covered. Unfortunately, no one could take a picture, we couldn't bring our phone but it was true, everything was here.

The children ran back to the where we were sitting. Their eyes were wide and glazed at what they saw. And all of us were surprised, we were the only people on this whole train.

We saw others jump on the train before going into the gate and there were a lot of people jumping on board to travel to their destinations. It took about twenty minutes. The captain of the train came out to greet us. "Hello everyone, how is your day? Welcome aboard, we hope everything here is what your needing for the trip we're about to take. This will be a day and a half trip. We have sleeper rooms for everyone here." He went on to say "if you notice, you're the only ones on this train …

I was talking to the conductor and he took his hat off and said "It's an honor to take your family to where we're going and the cause to protect America. I'm wishing you the best training in the world and your family to remain out of harm's way". Then he put his hat back on…He said, "I'm going to go down the aisle to collect all the tickets from the passengers.

" We all looked at each other to say doesn't he know there are only four of us here. He pulled out a punch ticket instrument to punch our tickets and then he said, "Just joking" and he pointed to all four of us as he walked away and vanished.

About ten minutes later we hear a voice come over the intercom. It said "Welcome, we're about to leave in ten minutes and the blinds on the train will overlap the windows for about 1½ hours as we move forward. We all looked at each. then the blinds from nowhere started overlapping the train windows and it went dark then lights came on from every area of the train.

It startled Hannah a little bit. We were taking everything in, then mini televisions turn on. There was everything on the train. Then it basically played relaxing music when the train started pulling off from the track. We were thinking they did not want others to see us on the train and hide any clues as to where we were going. This is the reason why the blinds come down. When they say top secret they really mean it …

The train started moving at gear stages like a stick shift for a car. It seemed to move in 1st and 2nd gear for a bit, then it went to third gear. The blinds still down. We didn't speak much, we were all waiting for the next surprise on the train. Everything so far has caught our attention… All of us knew this train was not like others, even the feel of the train seemed like it was really light as it moved on the track. The air inside suddenly felt colder, then I felt something on my seat and I looked at my family to see if they had the same reaction.

All of us did. My son said "heated seats" on a train. There's a digital button where you can turn up or down for the right temperature. My wife gave me

the thumbs up. We were all seated as the train rolled fast on the tracks, we couldn't see what was going on outside we just knew we were going forward. Then 1 ½ hours passed and the blinds came up on the train and we could see landscapes of trees flying by us.

The conductor told us over the audio that we could now move around freely. "You are on a new technology type of train where the exterior of the train blinds inside with the surrounding we call this the 'Invisible Train'.

I could not believe what he said, "Invisible Train? I can see other trains, their-car swipe around the corner and he was right, that trains blend in with the trees like we're not here. "Wow," I said my wife. "It's like a mirrored exterior. We're blending into the landscape, honey …"

All of us again looking around to see more surprises. We did not move from our seats at the moment.

Knowing the conductor told us we were free to move around the train cabin. All of us did not want to miss anything.

We were warm, all of us had TV's, and no one could see that we were on this train from the outside.

It was time to get some sleep. We went to a sleeper cabin to see what they looked like. It was great all had queen size beds and night stands. "You could live here if you wanted too, LOL," I told my wife Hannah.

She said "No honey, there's no way. It looks good but I need to have my own place that doesn't move at 250 miles per hour."

Sleep was needed. We stayed up as long as we could, trying not to miss anything. The morning came quickly. I woke up and walked around the train and I happened to look outside. There seemed to be a huge lake in front of us. I thought they're going to turn the train around this lake. It seems that I was the only one up at this time.

The train did not turn it kept going straight and I panicked like 'please tell me this train is going to turn' and my thoughts spoke out loud and I yell "We're heading for the water, brace yourself, everyone! Oh my god, we're going into the water.' Then I see in the beginning of the water, it seemed like a tunnel that went into the water and then under the water. I bent down with my hands over my head.

And the train just dropped into the water. "Whoa," I said. "An underwater tunnel for a train. Now I have seen it all." It was smooth I woke up everyone to see this. I told them we're in a tunnel under water. We all look at each in amazement and wondered how did they do that.

The tunnel seemed to be made a long time ago. I do not know if anyone knows but us and those who made it…The breathing was the same it didn't change, the window looked great, it was like we were in a huge aquarium, we could see fish, lake plants, etc. I tried to touch the window. I wished we had brought our camera because no one would never believe us if we told them.

We started to do the motion of a fish in the train, it was funny and we were all still in disbelief on what's going on. The train traveled the lake for a little while then it went up and out to the forest and we wanted more of this new way of traveling. My children yelled out more, more!

Now that's a wake-up called Mr. Johnson and I said: "yes it was…"

The train conductor spoke on the intercom: We hope you are enjoying the scenery and please walk around to the other cars on the train. We will be arriving in 45 minutes at the airport for the second half of your travels. Please have breakfast and relax …

****

Chapter 22

I was looking at the text and everything that Brent's family learned in New Jersey. He also knew he was texting him the information about the Tribes and history and was amazed at the vast size of the tribe there in that part of the US. Learning a lot about American History told or not told is great too, always interested in facts about history.

My wife started walking around the condo. She seemed to have a lot more energy and asked how Laura was doing. I told her she was fine. She said, "There is a lot we have to do. I'm going talk in my language to you and you

can just do the thumbs up sign or thumbs down sign if you disagree. You do understand me so you can talk to me in broken English."

"Okay then, let's talk." Laura was on the computer but she cracked her door to hear everything that was being said. She understood the language spoken and the English too.

Sandura said "First I want to say I love you Marc Dazet …and I told her I loved you too, Aradnus. Then she went on in her language "…Yg Vcnv Dcdmpe.

I said, "We did talk."

"Rjcte another Tceg here…Marc, yes I remember you told me they are here too. This Tceg is Ogcl."

I put the thumbs down. I said, "Mean as in they want to harm us? …"

She said "Yes".

I asked her what we should do now and Aradnus said, "We have to figure out a way to Uvqn them period".

"We must find them here", I replied.

She said, "Yes we must."

I told my wife she did not have to talk anymore, I understand. Then she went back to English.

Laura was in her room wondering if her parents were in danger. She thought what she could do to. She had always been a proactive teenager…Then she stood up to shut her door quickly as her Dad walked by. He knocked on her door. He was checking in on her.

"Are you okay in there?"

 Laura said, "Yes, I'm fine. Doing my homework Dad."

Then Sandura was in the living room and she noticed something new. She was able to read her daughter's thoughts from the other room. They told her when she was away that she would have more special talents, she could read her daughter's thoughts. She walked to Laura's room, knocked on the door and Laura told her to come in.

Sandura said "Arual, we all have to work as a team. Please do not do anything out of the way, okay?" Laura wondered how her Mom knew what she was thinking about.

Then her Mom winked and they both gave each other a hug and Arandnus went back to the room where Marc was sitting.

When my wife came back from talking to Laura she said to me, "I feel that Mr. Brooks from New Hampshire is an important link for us…Marc, your right honey," and then she walked away. I immediately texted Brent, "How's it going over there?" Brent texted back, "It's okay, did you get all of my texts?"

I said "Yes. Brent, do you think the UFO sighting that happened in 1966 in both locations in New Jersey and Pennsylvania have anything to do with the Native American Indians?"

I asked the question that Marc wanted me to ask …And the older guy replied to the tour guide. The question seemed to open up more doors that many Americans did not know. He went on to say that "Native Indians have known a lot about the history of those who fly in the sky. Their tribes have passed on history for years about the lights above. The Mayans, Aztecs, and Incas received visitors from other worlds. They have seen them for years. It's kind of a fact of life with them."

He continued with his story, "We are entering into a time transformation, to bring all races and barriers of religion together to unite people. He also mentioned Tah-Co-Pah "The Healer" would help. During that time, 1966 and today, the return of these UFOs are here to assist us through these times. As time paces forward, each year they will be making themselves seen more and more. Both visible and invisible. These beings have helped us on earth many times before. They depend on our survival because they need certain resources that are in abundance here and in turn, they help us out by finding solutions to world problems. Most of the times they're invisible. I have heard stories they can shift levels of vibrations so we can see them. There are new forms of energy on our planet and they will occupy and help us with this transition."

All of us had a blank look on our faces. We were blown away by the events and facts unfolded to us and it seemed like we were the only family who knew all of this. I texted all the information to Marc in Virginia. We ate more and were honored that they let us know all about their culture and about the future.

My wife whispered to me, "Thank you, Brent Brooks" and the twins were happy too…We were leaving to head back to New Hampshire in the morning with our helicopter pilot. We were full and took all of the gifts given to us at the special dinner.

As soon as we arrived at the Sheraton, the front desk person said someone called for you while you were gone and left a message. He gave me the paper with the message and it said: This is Rhonda Cayuga your tour guide from the Lenni Lenape Tribe, call us back ASAP! I immediately took my cell phone out to call, my wife and Nelson looked at me as if to say is everything okay?

I responded, "Yes, everything okay so far, I will know more after this call." The phone rang and instantly I hear our tour guide's voice, she said an Indian word first then, "Hi Mr. Brooks."

I said, "Hello, is everything okay?"

"Sure it is, the elder member who was talking to your family today wants to give you something very important. Can you back by?"

"Certainly, I can be there in 15 minutes."

"Okay, see you soon," and Rhonda hung up.

Chapter 23

I told my wife and Nelson what they wanted and my wife suggested I take Nelson with me.

The Hotel shuttle took us back to the Lenni Lenape entrance. Standing there waiting for us was Rhonda and the man who was telling us the stories this afternoon. He walked over to me and he looked back at Rhonda to translate for him; he said he wanted to give me something and he asked me to stop by the UFO sightings area at the reservoir. Then he handed me an item and I took it, he was still speaking while he gave me this item. Rhonda, still translating for him said to bring this item to the reservoir that I'm giving you. I agreed to stop before we leave in the morning. All of sudden he went into a dance from his culture. I waved to both them as I went back to the hotel shuttle. I said "Thank you again for everything" and I wave and I invited them to my place in New Hampshire. They agreed they would visit one day.

The next morning we were all packed and I asked the hotel shuttle before bringing us to the airport could they stop by Wanaque Reservoir. The shuttle stopped at the reservoir, I took the item given to me and held it in my left hand the whole time. We drove near the sign that said marked where the 1966 UFO sighting took place. I jumped out the car and as did Nelson and the rest of the family stayed in the shuttle.

I started walking to see why he wanted me to come here. I was outside the path that was there and walked near it, looking for something. I kept walking, then all of sudden my left hand started shaking, not from being nervous but

the item in my hands moved in small motions. I keep walking and they keep moving faster. I thought 'what in the world is going on?' The items seem to be making a buzzing noise, then I look on the ground and I see something in between the leaves, making a noise just like the item in my left hand. I dare myself to reach down to pick it up. I was still in the what's going on mode then. I reached down to pick it up, it had the same colors as the item I had, both white and purple and it seemed that I had the other half of the item on the ground.

It was like it was a piece of a puzzle of something. I looked at the item, it was buzzing too and I put the pieces together to see if there was a fit. And they did, and as I put them together, a purple light went up in the air and a blue light went to the ground. I looked at Nelson and he wanted to take the item out of my hand...I said "No no…"

The pieces stayed together with both lights. Then from the Wanaque Reservoir, something happened in the bottom of the ocean on the coastal waters in Florida. A rumbling sound and fish swam away in fear, something was happening. Then underneath the sand and seaweed, a ship appears, slowly moving up from the ocean waters moving for the first time in untold years.

The size of this ship from another world seemed to be 8.5 miles long and it was new for any human eye to see. Brent knew he had an important relic in his hand …even the ocean waters seem to say what is this in our waters. The ship did not rise to the top of the ocean, it stayed underwater. It seemed like the ship was waiting for the right time…I just stood there, knowing what just happened, everyone in the shuttle just stared at him in shock on what just happened.

The ship stopped moving and then lights circulated around the ship. It appeared like this was a plan of many years to happen. But from where?

The lights from the relic turned off and I just stood there in pause mode for five minutes and everyone stood too. Then I yelled out what just happened! The walk back to the shuttle was slow and the door opened and they helped him in and shut the door quickly and the shuttle sped off.

The helicopter flight home seemed to move slowly. Everyone was in a daze, including the pilot. I knew all the money I had won could not change the moments of having two lights in my hand on the Wanaque Reservoir.

Everyone landed back in Seabrook, New Hampshire safely. I wondered how I was going text what just happened to me. I'm just going text the reporter and tell the facts about that day. The text read "Marc you're not going to believe this" and Marc replied "Go for it, you would be surprised what I do believe …

I sent the text to Marc and while the text went through, Sundara felt the text that was sent and she walked straight to the room where Marc was and waited to talk. It seemed like she knew everything that happened in New Jersey.

She said, "There were two lights, Marc."

"Yes…

****

On the ocean, located on the gulf of Mexico, they're cleaning up an oil spill. Many will not know about it in the press about her and others not being from this planet. They have helped many times in unexpected moments to save earth from harm. Then a blue light came on her device and she opened it. The image was not too far from the spill and it showed a 7D image of a ship underwater. She was surprised and thought this is it time for me to go. She went to the leader of the mission and held a hand sign to tell them she would go and she was gone. Traveling in an earthly American muscle car to the Atlantic Ocean near Florida.

She tapped a button from the device that showed the ship's image and it gave more information. It said in her language it was a 2000-year-old relic from Triangulum Galaxy. She stared at the image as she was driving, looking at how the ship appeared and possible functions it might have… and thinking. She was used to being called on for major missions. This one is different, 2000 years makes this different and now on earth…

There's a long drive before getting to the locations, Yautja knew all events on earth start with her. She is from the Triangulum Galaxy, all beings from here have enhanced conditions for protection and defending those conditions. She has telepathic capabilities where she can mentally receive messages, she can restrict the movement of others minds…she understands all languages. This is why she is in the Gulf waters near Mexico. She also has the power to let other minds speak to each other.

She can tell by looking at the ship that it's from her planet of Fiwisho. She comes from a long line of warriors in her family. Examples of century insolvents from her genes.

Her people are warriors who will stop at nothing to make sure the mission is done. Her family history helped the first female athlete compete. It happened with a British Wimbledon Tennis player name Charlotte Copper. She helped during the Renaissance era, the Great Wall of China. Many events we have helped. This time our planet needed help from earth…

She punches the gas in the muscle car traveling from the Gulf of Mexico to the Atlantic ocean in South Florida.

Chapter 24

It took 15 minutes just like the conductor stated. The blinds of the train were down at the moment as we entered the train station. The blinds came up and we saw airplanes taking off into the air, we knew this would be the next leg of the trip. Hannah was ready, along with the children to move forward. We jumped out and there was a small travel cart there which had a luggage area. We jumped on the cart and they did not waste time with the Johnson family. The car went forward, we all waved at the train conductor to say thank you for a safe trip.

The travel cart reminded us of a Walt Disney monorail, again were on the cart moving at a pace to look around. I looked around the airport to see if I recognized the area. Their family has traveled to many areas. As I was looking around I was not familiar with this area at all. I thought is this was a new airport in the U.S. or somewhere…We came to a stop and we all jumped out and there was a person holding a sign that read "The Johnson's". We knew he was there to help us so we walked toward him. He looked to be of Asian descent. He said, "Hello, I'm looking for the Jensen's, hello." We knew he meant Johnson's.

We waved our hands all four of us and he told us to follow him and we did. It seemed like a flat walking escalator, we all followed our guide, he jumped on and there was no one on this moving, walking sidewalk but us. Again we were excited when we arrived at this area.

It seemed like an indoor private airport hangar. In the middle of the hangar, there was a modern looking airplane, the color seemed to be both black and white in color. The Asian man told us this is your airplane, please board. There were steps there so we started going up on an escalator format inside the airplane. All of us were amazed again. There were 5 flight attendants waiting for us as we walked into the plane. The one thing I noticed that was new about this plane is it had no windows.

I looked at Hannah and said, "There are no windows in here." She saw the same as she looked around before we went to our seats. I asked one of the flight attendants where are all the windows. They said there are no windows and it has the option to run on lithium batteries if needed. You're on one of the newest planes out here today. This one will not go into public use for another 5 years.

The attendant went on showing us the plane. "In here, every seat is good. Let me explain while I show you where your seats are. The inside has the look and feel of a jet. Yes, it is a windowless airplane." The attendant then asked me how we liked the train ride here and Nolan said that it was a cool train.

"Please get in your seats and I can explain more about this airplane." We rushed to our seats to sit down. I'm glad I did not get the memo on the travel itinerary, we all were into how modern everything is.

The attendants stood to explain everything. They went on the say that from here to your destination, you will arrive in ½, very quickly compared to a normal airplane…in a normal plane, it would take 5 hours …

I looked at my family to say "Whoa". The attendant went on to say that "the plane is designed with the first airplane projector screen on the ceiling and sides of the airplane with advanced LED modules." The lights turned off, all of sudden the hangar and the sides of the hangar were visible on the ceiling of the plane and the sides.

Then, the attendant said "The screen can change to many settings from the clouds we will fly over or any setting you want that is in our system". And all of sudden the screening of the hangar disappeared and it went to the regular ceiling in the airplane.

They showed us the exit doors and everything needed for safe travel. The attendant said "I will share more about what the airplane can do later within the ½ hour time. Please put on your seat-belt now." Then the plane started. Hannah, Zelda, and Nolan did what they were told, I was still thinking about what they demonstrated before the flight.

The plane started to move and had a private runway to leave for takeoff. We heard the pilot say "Thanks for flying the Oikola Telsla Aircraft". He coasted out the hangar to the main runway… There's no airplane in sight but ours. I had no clue how far advanced airplanes could be.

The pilot said "We're about the take off" and before he said the word off, the plane started moving at top speed and was off the ground into the air. A new type of speed I have never felt before.

All of sudden the plane went dim and the LED screen popped up beside me, it looked like a computer monitor where a window should be. It said "I'm your personal aviator, how are you doing Mr. Johnson? Can I help you with anything?" It was on screen and it showed me a menu of what I could choose from. Food to drinks, Go Flavor, Go TV, Hulu TV and on-demand movies. I saw a button that said settings where I could change the windowless setting to seven setting. One said current times, Rural, City, Small towns, Space, Moon, and Mars. The other three received their personal aviator, asking them what they wanted. Zelda asked her Mom if she could order a Pepsi, of course, she said yes.

What seemed to be a ½ hour airplane trip, we wanted to last for another hour. I clicked on current times and the window and the ceiling showed clouds flying by us, it felt like we were in Wonder Woman's Invisible Jet. My wife Hannah enjoyed the settings I choose for the ceiling and sides of the Tesla Airplane. Looking at the clouds go by as we were moving fast but the clouds seem to stay still as we flew by them. Nolan said, "What a sunroof we have!"

The attendant came back to our plane and said "I have a Pepsi here for the young lady. If you want to play games, there is a console here too. We have them here from RV, PS5, She went on to say "Your trip with us today will be short, you may not have time to try them all out but the option is there if you want."

The flight attendant asked them how they liked the view, we all clapped like we were at the Oscars.

A ½ hour went by again too quick, just like the train trip. We wanted more. The plane went back to windowless and dim light. The scenery lifted and the pilot's voice came over the intercom.

The pilot said, "We're at the location and we will be landing in 5 minutes." I turned to my wife and put both hands in the air like, "how was that for a ½ hour flight? We buckled our seat belts and the plane seemed to glide onto the landing strip, again this is the first time feeling this type of landing.

When our plane glided in it was so smooth. When we came to a complete stop a monitor on the side came on for us all and said in a digital format: **Thank you for flying with us today… Enjoy your time here and thank you for your service in the Army.** We all smiled and felt appreciated.

We deplaned and started to look around and again, we were in another airplane hangar and when I looked out there, a Hummer was waiting for us again. I noticed Colonel Mathews was on the driver's side. I thought I saw someone I knew but we just grabbed our things and started heading towards the Hummer.

Colonel Mathews said, "Good, you made it here safely. Normally I would have one of my soldiers pick you up but I wanted to be the first to welcome you here 2nd Lt Harold Johnson and Family." We all smiled and said thank you for this!

"Jump in, your luggage is safe and heading to the base. We have you covered. You noticed in your travels no others were around, just your

family." We nodded in acknowledgment and jumped into the Hummer. We were now anticipating what the outside world looked like.

****

I received a call from the newspaper from Amelia. She said "Mr. Dazet hello, ET phone home, do you know who this is?

I said, "Yes, this is Flo from Progressive Insurance telling me to pay my bill."

Amelia laughed, "Well Mr. Dazet I have a story for you to report. Come into the office for the details."

I told her I'll be there in an hour.

As soon as I got off the phone, I get a text from Brent and he was explaining what happened to him with the two lights in his hand. I froze and I read the text. I texted that I would get back to him later to get more details. Whoa I texted back about the lights.

Sandura hugged me and told me to be careful. While driving to work I was thinking about what happened to the Brooks family in New Jersey. Trying to put the pieces together and make sense of it all. I walked into the office, greeted everyone with high fives and hello's, and went straight to Amelia's office.

She said, "Wow look what the ocean brought in!"

I smiled and said, "There's a lot going on."

Amelia continued, "We received some information from Hampton, Va. from the NASA Langley Research Center. Can you drive up there to find out what they have for us?

I told I would take a drive out there for her. She went on to say "I'm giving you a Press Pass to interview one of the engineers over there at 3:30. Is that okay? Again I told her no problem.

I wonder what type of story they have for me to write. He thought to himself that this story seems to fit my life right now. Like a piece of a puzzle, he must have in his hand at a later date.

He went with his editor's hunch to go there. He thought, "Humm, Hampton, Va." It has been a while since he had been there he took his wife and daughter to Disney on Ice at the Coliseum there.

It was time for me to drive to the Virginia Peninsula. I told Amelia that I was heading out. I texted my wife to tell her I loved her. I was driving on the highways crossing into the Hampton Roads Bridge Tunnel and as I check the rearview mirror, I saw a truck following me into Hampton. I thought, "here we go again." I waited to see if anything would happen and all seemed clear.

The truck following me vanished for a moment, I kept forging ahead. On the other side, I saw a Hampton University welcome sign and I glanced at my gas.

gauge. The GPS showed that I was near the research center and I had just spotted a 7' 11 with gas pumps, so I drove in and parked in front of one of the pumps. I can hear 80's music from inside the store. I jumped in line and when it was my turn in line I noticed the two name tags. One said Dante and the other said, Crea. "Can I have $ 10.00 on Pump 2, please. Now filled up, I jumped in my jeep and made a right turn onto the main road and I'm here at the research center.

Chapter 25

I'm at the front of the research center in Hampton, Va. and there is a guard there. You need a badge to get in so I pull out my Press Pass that Amelia gave me from the paper. As I showed him the pass he said go ahead and that I could wait in this area. Someone will come down to bring me in. I was looking around, I knew this center was very historical for NASA and flight test of aircrafts. It opened in 1917 and had to be one of the first buildings open for NASA. I saw the sign that stated they're primarily an aeronautical research and space center.

I looked at the clock on the wall, I was there early to make sure I was on time. This is a trick I had to learn as a reporter when you interview people. Their time is valuable and you have to respect that as a seasoned reporter.

All of a sudden a door opens and a person with a beard and glasses came down and said: "Hello Mr. Dazet?"

"I said "Yes."

"Hello, my name is Dr. Eugene Brooks. (I thought to myself his last name sounds familiar) I'm a fan of your work at the *Virginia Pilot*."

" You are?"

He said, "Yes, you know my nephew."

" I do?" And then it hit me, the last name "Brooks" He is Brent's uncle. He's the one Brent was talking about in New Hampshire who gave him the satellite coordinates to view the channel.

"Yes, he's my nephew, he just won the Lottery in New Hampshire."

I said, "Yes we're friends."

"Come into my office," Dr. Brooks ushered me inside.

As I followed him down the hallway, I see pictures of aircraft on the wall from the past to current space aircraft and pictures of people. I know not many people have the chance to even be in the building, I heard the security is pretty tight with the positive research being done here.

We are walking and he takes a turn, all the doors are shut but for maybe one or two. I thought I've always wanted to know who his uncle worked for because of the information of the satellite directions. Then I thought he wants to talk to me all of sudden. Does he think I know something or is something wrong? I will soon find out.

We came to his office and he shut the door behind him. There were many degrees on the wall and awards. He really earned his way to being a doctor. He offered me a seat and began to talk about his nephew, Brent. He said "The story you wrote about my nephew, very good. He loves his family so much_-

he is willing to give his earnings to future families that are not here yet on earth. Who does that? Do you know anyone who would do this with their Lottery earnings?

I said, "No, this was why I took the flight to New Hampshire to interview him. I had to find out for myself and tell everyone".

"You're wondering why you've been invited you here, aren't you?"

"Well, yes I am," I replied.

He asked me if I had some questions to ask him and me-. I most certainly did. "I thought if I ever got a chance to see you, what would I ask, and here it is my chance to ask. How did you know which coordinates to show your nephew about the navigational markers, Dr. Brooks and the term Triangulum Galaxy? Exactly how did you know?"

He went on to say in a low voice …"Do you know what time travel is?"

I was alarmed when he said this. "Yes, I have heard of it. I saw the movie Back to the Future when I was a teenager."

He said, "Well, do you believe that it is real?"

The reporter from Virginia paused and said: "I never met anyone as a reporter who has talked about this subject."

He continued, "Time travel is very regulated and kept very tight, many know about it but only a select few have access to this technology. Time travel has been around for a long time. When it was first implemented there were problems in the earlier programs but nowadays it is much better and tightly controlled. Have you experienced or said the word Deja-vu?"

 I answered, "Yes, hasn't everyone?"

And then Dr. Brooks went on to say, "This is a small vibration in time travel that happened. Each section of the world is accountable for their time travel, there are companies that have regular workers and others who are higher levels who are time travelers. Most of the workers who are working do not know of the other people at that company, it functions like a regular company."

I did not take notes this time, I just listened to what was being said. Then I asked what every reporter would ask at this very moment, I asked, "Are you a time traveler?"

The Dr. looked at me and did not say a word, he shook his head yes but did not say yes. He just keeps talking about the parameters of this subject.

When he nodded yes I knew it he was telling the truth because of my wife Sundura. I knew the unbelievable could be attained.

"There a lot which has happened to my nephew in the past two months, yes?"

 I said, "Yes there has." I knew because Brent had texted me the events in New Hampshire and New Jersey.

He went on to tell me, "Everything that has happened is for a reason…

My nephew knows me as his uncle. And it's true, I am. There is a side he doesn't know of me but you do now as a person from a different time. I'm a window of time 50 years in the future. I will name a few items that will come from my time…Everyone there is fluent in every language. We have a Colony on Mars, there are electronic noses for weather patterns in advance…Our clothes and jackets are climate controlled."

I was lost in thought listening.

"The drones you're seeing will play more major roles in the future of farming and news stories." He continued, "Marc, have you heard about the invisible trains and windowless airplanes yet during this time?"

Marc shook his head, "No I have not."

"This is too soon for the public to know. I'm giving you a glimpse of the present but mostly where I am from…

"Before all of this happens there are others from other planets who are in need too. Some will be nice and others not so nice if they don't get their way. I'm preparing my nephew for these very moments and your part of this is to help, Marc. To help all of us advance and for your protection, I'm going to give you a special number. You can call this number anytime in life and it will reach me anywhere. Or if you have anything to say or wanted to tell me, use the number, but you must promise not to tell my nephew who I am."

"Promise me," he said and without hesitation, I promised. "This number is interchangeable, meaning you call the year that you're in. This year is 2017 first four number 2017 then the next numbers the current month 11th and the present day 26 then it will ring straight to me 20171126. Your present year, month and day this will be how to connect…

"Okay well, I think we have talked a lot today. Thank you for coming here, Marc."

 I didn't know what to say back...it took me a while to say Thank You. I think if I was any other person I would have walked out as the story began. I knew better though, that the truth was spoken to me. We, reporters, find truths, this time truth found me.

I stood up and shook his hand and he walked me to the lobby. I returned my badge and slowly walked to my Jeep to head back home. My wife texted me, "Honey, are you okay over there?" I text back "yes" and said I would see her when I'm home for sure.

What a day…I saved the format of the numbers on a small piece of paper and stored it in my wallet. Driving back home, the speed limit was 70 on the highway. My mind was going way over the speed limit.

I made it home safe and Sundura was there to greet me and my daughter just got back home. My wife gave me a hug and she started toward the living room. Then she stops in her tracks and turned around to stare at me. Then she kept walking and Sundura thought to herself, "Who is this Dr. Brooks and what is his motive about his nephew." They told her that she would be able to read thoughts with time and they were right. It's starting to show up little by little.

I asked Sundara if she was okay she said: "Yes I am, my husband …"

****

Dr. Eugene Brooks, the name written on his desk, looked around the room and seemed eager to move forward. He jumped up from his desk and walked down the hallways to a room which was very open. It had huge glass in front with the listing the different time zones in the room and the Dr. checked his watch. He saw the time 5:00 pm eastern time zone; in London 10:00 pm; in Tokyo, it's 7:00 am...He thought to himself that before the time zone everyone had their own local time zone based on the sun "Solar Time".

The UK was the first to adopt a time zone, then the US followed next with four different time zones. The country of China has the same time zone…He thought where he comes from the time zone is based on the seasons, in the winter there are 3 time zones and in the summer there 5 times zones.

The International Space Station time zone, where there is less gravity, the time moves faster than any of earth's time zones. He thinks about the how GPS satellites work for those traveling in the automobile and time travel for directions. He started walking outside towards his car, waved to the guard, and Dr. Brooks hopped in the car and drove away.

****

I decided to text Brent to see how he was doing and keep his promise to his uncle to remain close with his family in Seabrook, New Hampshire. I text him and ask "How was the trip?" Brent texts me back that he was "in the helicopter heading back home with his family and he wrote everything has been intriguing…"

I replied, "Yes, I've always thought the Native American India culture know more than we know about visitors from another galaxy. Brent agreed and said he took a picture of the relic he had found in New Jersey.

I looked at the picture on my phone I thought I've never seen anything like that. He said he will show me more when he gets back to Seabrook. I was about to text him about his uncle then I stopped myself.

****

Everyone seemed very tired on the helicopter while enjoying the trip back home. Margret was wearing some clothing from the Lenni Lenape tribe which she was very proud to wear. The twins were up, looking out the window and still excited about this trip and awesome ride. Jarvis and Jerry are known to answer each other's sentence when speaking to others … Nelson seemed happy to go back home too. Myself, I was thinking what next after I saw that light in my hands. I was thinking was that a sign for us or another person or planet. He put the relic in his pocket, looked over to Margret and his twins, thinking I hope I'm not in some type of danger…

Chapter 26

We didn't travel too far in the Hummer before we saw the entrance of the base and the sign read:

Welcome To the Space Marine Infantry

below it read

Operation Space Sahara 20 then

"Above And Beyond". We knew we were on a base, but not where it was. Usually, our family knows the location of the base, the state, or country. This time there was absolutely no clue. We see in the distance an ocean, and as the Hummer keeps driving, just like at the base, he received his briefing ion there where many domes everywhere. Some large, some small and were on top of each other like poles stacked in fives. It was the most domes I had seen in my life at one time and these weren't the type of domes I normally saw. They were made from the outside, it seemed, with a very different material that I had never seen before and there were infantry platoons marching in cadence. I looked at Colonel Mathews to tap the window down so we could hear outside and he agreed in silence to hear the marching cadence.

We heard "Let'em blow let'em blow, Let the four winds blow, Let'em Blow from the east to the west. The SpaceBorne Marines is the Best, Standing tall and looking good, Ought to march in Hollywood. Hold your head and hold it high, Space Marine Platoon is marching by."

There were more words. I tried to hear in the car as the Hummer kept moving by…Then we arrived at a dome-shaped home and in front of the home said Space Marine 2nd Harold Johnson and family. I thought this must be our home.

I looked around to see the other homes, they looked similar in size, we knew this did not change wherever we went. The Colonel said "This is your new home. Welcome to the base." Our family looked at each other he continued to say, "You see this Hummer. This Hummer, normally a gas car, which is yours to use by the way, but here on base all cars and vehicles are electric."

He walked near the home and he said, "The key to open your front door and everything else on the base is your heartbeat and hand recognition.

This is the key to every area of the base, certain domes will open here for your mission only, your family will have access to the public dome and your home is secure for all of your family's heartbeats and hand. To open and close the doors…Think of it like if you had keys on you those keys are different for all family members and some the keys are the same."

"Please look around your new home, your moving truck will be here tomorrow." He walked us to the door and the Colonel said, "Go ahead and try." So I went close to the device on the outside of the dome house. All of sudden a small window opened up and there was a green light that said opened and I opened the door and we all walked in. At this moment we weren't inside the home yet. We were in a medium size small room. I saw another door which was the main door to go into our home. When the first door shut, there was a green light that came on for the second door to open.

"Go ahead and go see, you guys." We went in and all of us felt like we were on the show HGTV Home. All of us looked at each other and just yelled "Wow" looking at this, the circle's space looks really trendy. The Colonel told us these type of Dome homes are made from a material we have studied for a long time which can withstand hurricanes, tornadoes and all types of metal including armor.

"2nd LT Johnson, we will have more briefing on the bamboo, glass, and metal you guys are seeing everywhere. This helps us in many ways for training."

I understood what he was saying right away. "There are other items in which it protects itself I will explain in the briefing." I understood. The Colonel continued, "All dome-shaped buildings on this base have the same exterior protection, for weather and training." All of us looked around at each other as if to say it's about time and how did they invent this?

"You noticed there is no plastic here. We have a certain type of wood and metal shipped in. The wood is shipped in from New Hampshire and various locations and this certain type of wood lasts a long time and absorbs waste…You will see this type wood and bamboo in certain Domes and others you will not. Please look around there are many windows small and big to have a feel of the outdoors and you click this button and it can go back to wood. The windows are made in a triangle shape, each room will have control buttons first until we show you more advanced ways for your home; right now your formula is with buttons. These homes feed off of the weather made with thick stone on the outside and wood and metal on the inside.

He said "I'm not going give you guys a tour, I want you to look around and explore for yourself your new surroundings. Your items will be here Wednesday afternoon and a briefing will be on Friday. You'll need some time to settle in. I'll meet you at my office then and I'm not telling you where my office is located. This will help you learn the new facilities better."

There temporary furniture here until tomorrow for your family needs. I was in my civilian clothes as I reached over to shake his hand and my wife and children gave him the thumbs up sign and he went on into the small room to exit the dome.

Again we were amazed at the sheer size of the place, one area of the home had an archway made of a certain type wood. It expanded on the left side and right side of the arch into the library. It had all type of books there from our past and the present times. I thought to myself, I'm glad books still exist where we are located now… My wife was in the living room and saw eight windows in a row to look out into your backyard. Most of the space seemed to spread out everywhere. We went to a door that looked like an elevator there was an area to wave your hand and I did.

A computer voice said, "Entrance please…" We all jumped in and after Zelda jumped in the door shut automatically and we went downstairs and the same space upstairs was downstairs. There was a pool table and game room, the likes we have never seen before. Basically, we just peeked our heads out of the elevator, all four of us, looked around and decided to head back upstairs. Our thoughts were to just sit in the living room and rest a bit and start the tour back in the main area.

Colonel Mathews drove the Hummer to his office. He went by the building and building door just opened up for him to enter and instead of going into the main building. The floor started moving up to a second floor and he waited. Then he opened the second door to go to his office, was saluted and walked to his office and scanned something on the desk and a female voice came over the intercom.

"Did they make it in safely Colonel Mathews?" He spoke back to the voice and said they did. The voice sounded familiar, it was the lady at Fort Riley, her voice came over. She said, "Are you sure he is the right fit for the SpaceBorne Marines Unit?" She went on to say "I thought he was a better leader for the (PMR) Planetary Marines Reserves." The Colonel said he could have been in that unit too.

She said, "Many are not use to having All Female Platoon leaders for that regimen."

He replied "Times are changing here. That platoon is training on the moon and you have the best trained female leaders. They are good with space and each as tougher than any five guys together.

I know it throws a lot of new recruits for loop as soon as they're on the moon for the (PMR) but they will get used to it."The voice responded, "I trust your judgment, you need a good team being the first to go on any mission."

"Yes, your right."

"Okay, talk with you soon Colonel."

He said okay, then a voice said completed. The Colonel stood up, went to an area of the room and he spoke to an empty space. A purple vision appeared, it looked like a digital folder. The front said "Training".

****

I was sitting here thinking what a trip to New Jersey we had. I hugged my wife Margret and thanked her for going. The twins seemed happy to learn so much about the Lenni Lenape Native American culture. I went over to talk to them and asked, "Did you guys have a great time?" Both of them said yes. They wanted to stay longer.

"How about we invite them here one day?"

Both shouted in agreement, "Yes indeed!"

"I need to talk to you guys. The main reason is about that beam you saw coming out my hand. Please do not tell anyone in school what you saw. It's extremely important we keep it between us." They both agreed.

Jarvis asked me what did I think that meant. I told him I did not know yet and was trying to find out. " I'm stopping by the Free State office today, would like to come in and hear what they have to say?" They told their dad they had a mixed martial arts lesson today but the next time they would like to go.

I asked them about their teacher. Jerry said, "We're learning Japanese mixed martial art our instructor name is Atushi Sensei. We just call him Mr. Atushi."

"Yes, I heard he's really good teacher." Both Jerry and Jarvis agreed.

Margret was dancing to some of the Native American music in the living room, it seemed like she never left New Jersey, she's here but there. When we were there with the Lenni Lenape Tribe, we witnessed many dances there, each step has meaning. And all the types of dances had a name for it. My wife liked the Butterfly dance they performed. I told her as she was dancing, "I'm going stop to check on the Free State Project office.

When I was about leave, there a was an Asian voice on our intercom system. "Hello Mr. Brooks, can I talk with you. I'm the mixed martial art instructor. I wanted to have a few words with you before their lessons begin." Nelson heard all the words and he agreed that he was safe to come to the door. I beeped him to come to our home.

I wondered what he had to say to me. It took about ten minutes before the doorbell rang.

He saw Nelson first and did a small bow and he did the same to me and I bowed back, pretending to know how to bow to another. I respected this person before I meet because of Nelson.

He was wearing a loose coat and had a collared shirt on and he said to me, "Mr. Brooks, can I talk with you privately in your office?" I said sure so we went. I offered him a seat and he watched me sit first then he sat down.

He said, "I want to share some information with you, Mr. Brooks. You have given me the honor to train your sons in the mixed martial arts and I wanted to give you the honor of how I'm going to train them before they start."

I said with a smile, "How gracious of you to share with me for my own peace of mind."

Mr. Atushi goes on to say, "You have two identical persons, boys. In my country in Japan, there is a tradition on how to train two who are identical. First, they must never compete with one another or train together at the same time with each other. I will have them under the same roof but train with other people.

I thought to myself what a unique way of training._-

He continues, "You will see they are teenagers now, both of them will train with an older person instead of their own age. It is better that the older train with the younger and the younger train with the older. It helps to develop skills of strength and skills of restraint. When they grow up their mixed martial arts trainer will be with someone younger. I will be there and other instructors will be there to help them train correctly. Is this okay with you?"

And I, as their Dad thought about what he said and agreed. "Yes, that would be good Mr. Atrushi."

"They way we train, our concepts come from many forms. We want to train in this way," Mr. Atushi pointed to the painting on the wall in my office. He said, "There are many views to this picture in your office Mr. Brooks, you see the people who like the artwork have many views and opinions about the artwork. But there is another view from the artist who painted the art itself. **'You can either watch the art or be the art'**; both concepts are needed today, both help each other. This is what our training is about, to be the art." He paused when he said that to me in a lower voice.

I thought Nelson recommended a good instructor to our family. When he said the last phrase I looked around my office at the artwork and the concepts explained to me.

He then stood up and bowed to me to tell me he had to go. I stood to bow back and walked him to our door. He saw Jarvis and Jerry and he waved at them as he left.

Both the twins seemed puzzled to why he was at their home. Mr. Atushi Sensei jumped in his car and he left in an instant. Nelson looked at me not for protection, but for reassurance that we were in good hands with Mr. Atushi.

I waved and went back inside. I thought about the words told to me and I needed to make it to the meeting. I told Jarvis and Jerry, "You have a great person teaching you guys. I see you later this afternoon."

This was an important meeting. I asked Nelson to drive with me. Nelson is a part of the family now, he recommended Mr. Atushi for the twins. He didn't want to tell the twins who the recommendation came from.

And it was good to be protected in times like this. I need to thank my uncle for suggesting to have Nelson as our bodyguard. Before I go out the door I wondered what my uncle was doing these days. I took out my phone to call him "Hello Uncle Eugene".

"Well hello to you nephew," he said back. "How are you doing nowadays."

I said, "I've been doing okay. I just got back from New Jersey. Wow, what a trip."

" I'm glad you had a great time."

I didn't tell him what happened with the relic and light, not just yet. I said, "There is a great tribe there the Lenni Lenape."

Uncle Eugene said, "I know them very well. There is a large tribe in the Northeastern area, Delaware, New Jersey, New York, and Pennsylvania. Very huge, many do not know how huge they are. They're very connected to the past and the future nephew.

I was surprised my uncle knew so much about the Northeastern area… "Yes", he went on. "So how are the twins doing and your great wife Margret?"

"There doing great and the bodyguard you recommended is doing well too. Do you need any money or anything Uncle?"

" Nope, I'm fine."

"Okay Uncle Eugene, I wanted to call you on the way to a meeting. There's a lot happening since you gave me the satellite coordinates you know."

 He said, "Oh yeah, really?"

"Yes really!"

"I thought that would happen. Keep me posted on anything that happens, okay?"

"Okay, Uncle Eugene."

Chapter 27

Yautja, is driving to the east of Florida, almost there as she's flying down the road going 70 mph, a speed where she's from doesn't exist. She's driving to the coast of Pompano Beach Florida towards the Atlantic Intracoastal Waterways. She thought whether there is the same as the Gulf of Mexico. A little breezy with the blaze of the sun shining.

She doesn't waste any time, she is about 3 miles from the oceanfront and again looks at the location in the ocean of the spaceship on her image device. She thought I have to drive past Pompano to the nearest port to check my device and it said Port Royale in Fort Lauderdale and take a cruise ship up to Pompano Beach. She changed her directions slightly further down for the drive …

It must have taken her about 1 hour but there she was. Her shape blends in with humans. Instead of talking in Spanish, she switches to English and the guard at the port gate said,

 "Yes, do you have a badge to come into the port?" and she said no. Then she blocked his thoughts and reversed his thought back to let her go in and the guard said, "You can come in, is there a ship you're looking for?"

She said, "Is there any cruise ship that goes north to Pompano Beach, FL?"

"Yes," he said. "There's a cruise ship going there at Terminal A."

She said thank you, he waved her on in and she went straight to Terminal A.

There was a cruise ship there in the waters just like the guard said and she jumped out of here car and walked towards the Terminal. Staff members were there to ask for her travel tickets and she again reversed the thinking of two staff members as she walked on board in minutes with no luggage in her hands.

She noticed how the people were so happy. She had never been on a cruise ship in her life but knew about them from her studies. Inside she was really nervous about how people were acting. A lot of smartphones and picture snapping. This ship had everything in it, being the first time on a human cruise ship, she thought. It's cool what they provide for others.

Walking around like she was lost but alert, asking questions about this and that as the ship started moving out slowly. Everyone cheered, she could hear claps in the air. People were truly happy.

A half hour passed and by then she slipped out from the crowd and they were nearing close to the Pompano Port area. She went to the top of the ship and she tapped her hand and a type of futuristic suit came over her and she jumped off the cruise ship rail right into the water. The cruise ship kept moving towards the port as she swam away from the shoreline.

The suit from her galaxy seemed to move her faster and she could breathe in the water longer than any human. She went up to look for navigational markers in the water, for the locations of the ship below the ocean waters. She saw the markers and she knew she was close by…

She went to the area and there were louder sounds coming from her device. It made a loud sound and she looked around the surface of the water and dove straight down. A light from the suit she was wearing came on and she kept going down deeper into the Atlantic Ocean until she came upon what she was there for. She had never seen this type of ship from her planet before but she knew it was theirs.

The ship was floating into the water. There was a lot of space between the ship and water. She could see a circle in the center of the ship. She swam almost to the bottom of the ocean floor and she touched the device and all of sudden that circle moved and a beam of light hit the waters. She was underneath the light and all of sudden the light lifted her up in the air in the water. It was remarkable to see and she was going up into the ship in the deep ocean waters…

****

Sundara walked into her daughter's room to check on her. She said, "Laura you are part your Dad and part me."

Laura said, "I know".

"How was school, the people, they're treating you okay?"

Laura said, "Yes, now they are".

Sundara then asked her daughter, "Are boys chasing you now honey?"

"MOM," Laura said. "A few have made pass at me. But I'm more into studying now."

Sundara was proud when she said that. "If you ever have any trouble you can come talk your Dad and me at any time."

Then Laura said to her Mom, "I'm sorry but my door was cracked the other day and I overheard something."

Sundara perked up, "You did? What did you hear honey?"

She asked, "Are we in some type of danger or something?"

"No, we're not" she went on to say. "Your Dad did a story on a family in another state, they won the lottery there. And when you win something like that a lot can happen, good and bad."

 Laura said, "I heard about him be followed. Mom, you can tell me things. I want to help."

"Concentrate on your studying, honey. I know you have the same traits as I do, a very active person just like myself. I want to tell you something. Laura, be careful about changing climates in front of people. There's a time to do this and time not to…I had to learn this myself. I want you to know that when I had to go home to my planet, they gave me more skills of reading and shaping thoughts…I'm new to these type of skills, just like it's new for you with climates. It doesn't happen all the time. At this moment I do not know what your thoughts are. I wanted you to know this."

"Talk with you soon Laura." She gave her Mom a thumbs up. As soon as she shut the door, Laura wrote down something in a notebook.

I was on the phone with my managing editor Amelia, "How was the story Marc with the NASA Research Center in Hampton."

"There wasn't any story Amelia. He's the uncle of the person we wrote the story for, Brent in New Hampshire. He just wanted to thank me for a good story and introduce himself to me that was all."

… Sundara was listening to the conversation and she knew better from her thoughts.

I kept talking to Amelia, she said "We have to get another story from you, Marc. If you see anything tell and I will look for something for you to report."

"Okay, talk you at the office, Amelia."

I clicked my smartphone and again Sundara tried to read his thoughts, nothing again. She said, "Honey are you okay?"

" I'm fine."

"You seem different. I know you well Marc."

" Nope, I'm fine."

 Sundara knew something was wrong or puzzling. He wanted to keep what happened in Hampton quiet for now…

****

I thought to himself "time travel", I don't want anyone in our condo to be alarmed with their gifts they have and this was not the right time to talk... I had a small police and fire scanner on his desk to hear local news events live in the area. I was sitting there listening and there was the basic local news: fires, fender benders, someone was driving backward on the expressway in Virginia Beach…

I decided to head to the office. It was Thursday and it was again the day to choose a random newspaper and see news stories from other areas. I went in my Jeep to and arrived at the office in no time. I said hello to everyone and walked directly to the room where the newspaper scrolls were located.

I picked the newspaper from Pompano Beach, FL. I was thumbing through the newspaper and this headline caught my eye:

PERSON JUMPS OFF A CRUISESHIP IN MOTION

I keep reading. It had a picture of the cruise ship and two feet leaping off the boat in the water. I thought someone must have snapped the picture while they were on vacation on the ship. I wanted to do more on this story. I needed to ask Amelia about this, I have a reporter's hunch about this. Walking to the managing editor's office, I see Amelia on the phone.

She takes the phone away and says, "What's going on Dazet?"

I tell her I have another story I want to report on. Amelia forgot she was on the phone and said: "YOU DO?"

I said "YES" real loud and she signaled me that we need to talk about this she'll meet me at my desk in ten.

I took the newspaper scroll from Florida with me to my desk and was thinking what are the right words I can use to go on this trip and report the story…

Ten minutes on the dot Amelia shows up in my office and says, "Okay, what's up Marc?"

" I want to report on a story in Florida."

"Another road trip? We're a local newspaper for Hampton Roads, we report the news on seven cities: Virginia Beach, Norfolk, Hampton, Suffolk, Newport News, Portsmouth and Williamsburg VA."

I said, "Do not forget to say Chesapeake, Amelia."

She looked at me like I was trying to be smart.

I said, "Well, how about the Lottery story in New Hampshire?"

"Many people liked the story, Marc."

"Yep and many will trust me when I have a hunch about this story."

"Okay, how about you do most of the story here in Hampton Roads and if you really have to go, then I will book you an airline ticket. Where is the story, Marc?"

"It's in Pompano Beach, Florida."

Amelia said, "Let me read this story and I will get back to you in the morning Marc. Okay? In the meantime, see if you can get a lot of the info from here."

" Okay, but I think I need to be there. I just have a feeling I may miss out on something if I'm not on the ground asking people and looking around."

I was driving home from work when I received a call on the phone from Amelia.

She said, "that they want you to stay near here in Virginia for the story."

My speed limit went slower as I was driving. "Really?"

"Yes," she said, "They are looking at it like you're the new star of our newspaper and they want to protect you here."

"I understand."

Driving home I was thinking of a way to write the story here and possibly leave without them knowing. But right now I'm going listen and stay here in Virginia.

I knew I could get a better story on the ground. Maybe I can have someone help me there like an assistant. The speed limit picked up to normal as he made his way to the oceanfront back home to his wife and daughter.

Chapter 28

2nd LT Harold Johnson felt he made the right choice by deciding to take the assignment at an unknown location. He told Hannah, "I can't believe we're here." She agreed as they opened a door and it looked like their new garage and inside was two new types of cars. They heard about this car in Kansas but this seemed more advanced. Hannah wondered where the keys for the car to open the door were. She walked around the car and she saw a word on driver side window, it said 'Touch Window'.

The name of the brand of car one was by Ford/Google make and the other make, it was called Havel. Harold remembered reading about Havel, they're from Japan. Both cars were very advanced. Hannah stayed in the garage while Harold saw a purple button on the outside of the garage. It was labeled Cars and it blinked. He pushed the button, then all of sudden a holograph dome came over him. It looked like a demonstration video of the two cars.

He did not know which button to tap first. He called his wife to the area and she went inside the holographic dome to see the demonstration. They were both in awe. Harold asked his wife which button first, the Ford or Havel? He tapped the Havel because his curiosity wanted to know what this new car was about.

Then the dome went dark, a word came on in English, it said welcome to the Havel Demo.

Both of them just looked at the dome demo and the voice and they had to adjust their heartbeat to understand what was going on. The demo showed the car and a person put their palm of their hand on the car and it took a picture of the person's face as a key to get into the car.

Then he demonstrator jumped in and he drove the car to a location in the middle of the road near an office. He exited the car, then the demo went to the rim of his car and the rim of the wheel seemed to move and produce what seemed to be a Hoverboard. The man jumped on the board and it took him to the office and then the car parked itself. Just like that.

Not a sound was made while the demo kept going, it was like it was the first time seeing the future and they could not believe it. The next scene in the dome showed a mother and a child at a building, then at the office, the man tapped a glass display and it said car. Then another car at the office, a company car, drove itself and it was sent to pick up his wife and child.

Both Hannah and Harold looked at each other and said "No Way" at the same time. They kept looking, the second car picked up his wife and son and they put their hand print and face recognition on the car window like a key and the door opened and they jumped in. Their son touched the window of the ultratronics display glass window in the car. All of a sudden the car window went to another shade of tint.

The demo showed the wife and buttons on a display, there were two buttons for the highway route and the scenic route. They choose scenery to take them home. Harold said to his wife, "We're definitely not Kansas any more honey." She agreed. Then in the demo, the husband clicked a button at the office to see if his wife and son made it into the Havel car safely.

When they were close to home she sent something that came from the top of the car. It looked like a drone of some sort, it left the top of their car to go to their home as security. Then she tapped a button. While in the car, she turned on the home functions. Then the demo showed them arriving home, the mom and son were home safely and the drone went back on top of the car.

Harold looked at the car in the demo and ran out of the dome holograph to see if they had the same car in their garage. "Yes" it was the same car as the demo and he smiled at the car in joy. He ran back and his wife said out loud "Honey the man at the office drove the car back home. He was tired and took a nap and the car kept going. It drove itself while he took a nap, Harold." Then he made it home to his family. Harold was there and Hannah ran out of the demo to the Ford/Google car. This time Harold stayed in the demo. She didn't try the Havel car yet because she was fascinated with what she saw and decided to go with the American make first. She touched the window with her fingers and the door opened up, She looked around for more touch devices and asked Harold, "Do you think we're in California?"

Harold said "No way we are there, but it looks like it huh. So this an electric car."

Hannah said, "I have to get used to the new type of cars. I'm still a bit old-fashioned when it comes to cars."

Harold said, "New fashion needs old fashion too, honey."

Zelda and Nolan keep touring the dome home, running around like kids in a candy store. Each having their own room and virtual reality, Zelda said, "Wow, there are gloves here with the VR gear and Hololens glasses We will have to try it out later. I can't sit still right now, let's keep looking around."

The night fell on our new home quickly…Harold had a meeting scheduled with Colonel Mathews in the morning and without knowing which building his office was in. This was meant for me to become more familiar with the base.

7 am is still 7 am at any location. The sleep at the new place felt like they were on vacation. In the closet on a hanger, there were new color fatigues. The same infantry clothing he saw on the video monitor in Kansas, this time his name was on them with a patch on the arm. The patch had black wings and in the middle three red rectangles attached in the middle of the wings.

There was a ranking on the uniform that said SpaceMarine 2nd LT Harold Johnson, then there was a patch on left side of the fatigues that said 'Operation Space Sahara 20'. The hat had the space marine badge in the middle.

He went to the new car and remembered exactly what his wife did to the windows to open the car and it worked for him. The door opened and he jumped in and he waved his hand over the steering wheel and it started. There was an optional button for self-driving and manual, should he choose manual.

Self-driving is new for him, he put his hands on the steering wheel to back up and all of sudden a garage door opened and he backed the car to another garage door and a voice said, "Move back please" and he did and the first door shut and the second garage door opened up and he was on the road.

He saw all kinds of cars with colors he had never seen before. There were camouflage electric cars, he saw the cars that were orange, purple and neon. He thought this must be the future. Looking in his rear view mirror it seemed like he saw a car that changed colors before his eyes. Like it was mood paint, it was cool Harold thought that it looked like a butterscotch color on that SUV.

Finally he focused on finding Colonial Mathews' dome barracks. He can hear infantry chants marching by. Looking at the layout of the base he thought to stop in front of the building to see if he can ask around. A soldier came out of the building and he asked "Do you know where I can find Colonial Mathews," and the soldier looked at his badge and said, "Nope I don't."

The soldier seemed like he knew but was told not to tell anyone fresh on the barracks how to find places.

He stood in front of the building and thought the heartbeat sensor would open the door and it didn't. Thinking how can this happen, then he had an idea.

He parked and waited for a platoon to run by and he would pretend to jog with them to show everyone that's he not new. He heard the person leading the Cadence, "Go Left Right" and the soldiers would say "Sahara" Go Left

Right "Sahara" then he heard "A long long time ago, "I heard it on the radio" the soldiers repeated this. "I heard it on the radio" Then he said, "Left right Ye He Yaa". Then he repeated, "long long time ago and then 2nd LT Harold Johnson jumped in line and repeated the cadence "I heard it on the radio". Then he heard "it sound so good to me, US Sahara SpaceMarine". So he said, " One Guided Infantry".

Harold chanted back " One Guided Infantry". Then the cadence leader said, "Go Left Go Left, Go Left Right", they yelled "Change". The last item spoken was "Company halt".

After a while he asked one of the soldiers, "Man, Colonel Mathews moved his office" and the soldier said, "No he's still in the Evergreen building" and that's what he needed he slip out of the group, found his car and looked for the Evergreen building.

He looked inside the car for a digital map on one of the touch window buttons. He found the map and he drove to the directions he saw and made it. He scanned the building with the heartbeat sensor and a palm print option and the door opened up. He made it.

In New Hampshire, Brent had stopped by the main office of the Free State Project. He passed by the sign with a Porcupine and the words "Liberty in Our Lifetime". Brent had signed the statement of intent back in 2001.

Now in 2017, there are more than 20 thousand participants on board. There was a lady standing in front of the room talking to people sitting down. She waved at Brent when he walked through the door and he waved back without interrupting her. She said to the people, "There are many of our members in the New Hampshire House of Representatives, they only serve for two years.

The meeting ended and the lady walked over toward Brent and said, "How you doing, long time no see since you won the big prize. We didn't know if you would come back here."

Brent said, "I will always be a part of the Free State Project when it comes to the rights of the people. I'm a Free State Project member period. Is there anything you want me to do, this why I came by?"

She thought about what Brent said. "We were thinking of setting up a type of a currency for those who joined and we may need your help to start the program. More people are moving here and I thought it would be great to have a community currency here in New Hampshire."

Brent thought about the idea and said, "What a good idea. Have other communities tried this type of project?

She said, Yes, we have studied this, they have tried this in many California, Colorado, and Michigan. This is for the those who move here and live here."

"That sounds like a good idea," Nelson said.

Brent said, "Look, I have an Indian Tribe I want to dedicate the new currency to, the Lenni Lenape Native American."

She thought about it. "Okay, you have a deal…You help us with the project."

"Deal, how much money do you need to start?"

She said, "I'm not sure, I will do some research and find out more…" Brent was proud that he was helping with this idea for the Indian tribe and thought "I can't wait to invite the Lenape people here to Seabrook, NH."

Something triggered from their trip there, the relic found, and the lights at a location in New Jersey. (why is this hanging here?)

He said goodbye at the main offices and headed home to see his family. On the way home toward the New Hampshire shoreline, he noticed on one of the roads closest to his home, a dark purple truck trailing him. He told Nelson. Nelson went into overdrive, the truck went by Brent's car and disappeared. Nelson was in an "I dare you to try harm Mr. Brooks mode", he was ready if anything were to happen. Brent thought, this why you were hired for our family.

He made it home and a few minutes later the twins were in from their mixed martial arts lesson. Both of the chopping the air practicing different moves. Jarvis said to Jerry, "Watch this". Jerry instantly went into a stance.

Margret yelled at them to stop. "No more before I hand chop you both." The twins knew their limits with their Mom when she says Jar and Jer that means to stop it.

Brent told his wife what happened at the meeting about adding new currency and dedicating the idea to the Lenni Lenape Native American Tribe. Margret was really happy about that suggestion.

"I wonder if their sub-tribes like Turtle, Wolf, and Turkey would also like their own currency? Brent thought putting some of his winnings to good use would be neat.

Chapter 29

Sundara was looking through what seemed like a bag that was not from earth. Inside the bag were all types of items from her planet. It looked like foods and items for her favorite tea Zum-Zea Tea. There were a couple of items inside that she did not know what they were. She did not want to test inside the condo right now. She wanted to make her favorite Ooynt Salad. It's called the "Al Fresco". She opened something up and the color looked like a plant with a mix yellow and orange together. The second item was round and had the same texture of a pickle. She diced these items with the yellow and orange plant and there was her Ooynt Salad. Laura loved it too.

When she was done making the salad, Marc came through the door from the newspaper office with a confusing look. Sundara asked if he was okay. As she was staring at Marc, she thought to herself "I wonder why Marc wants to report on someone jumping from a cruise ship?"

Marc spoke. He said, "I wanted to do a story on a lady jumping from a cruise ship in Florida, but the managing editor will not let me go down to do the story. They want me to stay here for some reason."

"I thought me being on the ground is better…I'm thinking how can I still do the story? I know we have the internet, and smartphones but being there in person is better. It's like when you watch CNN, they always have a reporter at the scene there."

Then Sundara said, "Honey, your working for the *Virginia Pilot* newspaper, that's different than CNN."

He said, "I know they want me here to cover local stories. I do understand. I just have a hunch something is going on there. Why would a person jump off a moving cruise ship like that before they get into the port."

His wife thought about the questions and said, "You do have a point there, Marc."

He walked around and said, Never mind, I think I will pass on the story right now and find something local."

Now his wife was curious about the lady jumping all of sudden, too.

For the rest of the evening, everything seemed okay. Marc went back to his desk and was looking at the paperwork and remembered the envelope he received with the letter "M" on it. He opened it again and was looking at the blueprint plans left for him and he noticed on the corner the word QFGN. It looked like his wife's language.

He doesn't know how to speak Ooyntian. He understands it and he notices it when it's written down. He calls his wife Sundara in the room. She saw the blueprints before. Marc pointed out to her some words, he said, "Look right here on the corner, this word." She looks and she notices it right away.

She said, "This from Ooynt." She keeps reading the word and other words on there that she missed the last time. "These are blueprints to build a spaceship to go underwater."

Marc looked at her and she looked at Marc. "Yes, it's for building a ship that is supposed to travel."

Marc went into reporter overdrive. "You mean these types of spaceships. is it already built or it's suppose to be built now?"

Sundara said she did not know. "From reading what's there it looks like it has not been built yet, but I'm not sure."

Marc sat there for a while looking at the plans thinking who would know if this is supposed to be built for the present times?

Who would know? Sundara was pacing the room and she asked, "How did you get these plans, honey."

Marc said, "They were on my desk at work in an envelope left for me."

****

Chapter 30

Colonial Mathews looked forward to starting the day when there was a beeping sound at the door and the story slide opened automatically and there, in uniform, was 2nd LT, Harold Johnson walking in. He saluted the Colonel and he saluted back. He said, "You made it!"

Harold replied, "Yes I'm here." This room looked different than the one on

the barracks at Fort Riley, Kansas. There were a lot of screens everywhere, in the air, on tables… even on the floor.

He asks, "How do you like your new home and the base?"

Harold said, "My family is adjusting daily. We like the house and two cars."

The Colonel remarked, "Yes, I like a good old American gas car myself. I like both old and new, this why I still have my Hummer. I like technology too but things from the past are just as good when you need them."

2nd LT Johnson agreed. "I'm the same way."

The Colonel went on to say, "This is why you were picked because of your past stationed and your new school with old school ways. A rare person to find, you and I are. Don't lose those traits while your training here or on the field as a SpaceMarine."

He said, "I will not."

The Colonel continued, "Let's get to work, have a seat. Welcome to Operation Space Sahara 20. The domes are quite unique here. You will have access to enter many of them and others as your security clearance increases, so will the access to other domes here on the base. You noticed we have an ocean on one side of the base. The ocean is open to the public and sections use it for training. Basically, everyone here has a purpose to help you advance. If you see a lifeguard watching the ocean they're experts at swimming and rescuing others. Not many in the world know about this base

or its location. I want to meet your instructors. The screen opened up on top of the desk and there were three separate people there. "Hello, 2nd LT." Each one introduced themselves …One said, "I'm from the Spacebravo Backwards Commander Jorge Coleman," he saluted backward to the 2nd LT.

Then the next one said, "I'm Commander Kristin Hernandez from Spacebravo Moon Division." Kristin asked Harold, "Have you ever heard of a space elevator?"

Harold said, "No I have not." That was it, she stopped talking.

Then the last person who spoke, "We welcome you to the Space Marine training. I'm Commander Jacob Scott of the Spacebravo WaterSpartans…

They all welcomed him in, talked for a little bit and then they're screens vanished. Just then two people arrived in the room, They looked like civilians, it was a woman and a man, both older and both had folders. They shook my hand and said, "We want to welcome you to our base and want to share your lifestyles here, your living arrangements and items we want to point out."

Then another area opened and there was something I had never seen before. It was bamboo computer keyboard and monitor. The woman's name was Sally (I looked at her name tag) and the gentleman's name tag said, Dr. Eugene Brooks. He had a beard and glasses. He seemed not dressed for the current times like every else in the room.

The room went dim and this huge bamboo monitor came on. On the middle of the screen, it showed the picture of the base, people were moving and

Sally went on to say, "I bet you're wondering why we asked you not to pack plastic on this mission 2nd LT Harold Johnson for yourself and family?"

I said, Yes, I was thinking about that. It was kind of hard to do for our family."

Dr. Brooks said, "Well where you just came from there's a lot of plastic being used, it's everywhere. Yes?" Harold thought about what he said and he remembers the recycling and all the plastic they used and threw out of the home when they packed. It was a lot.

Sally said, "This base has no plastic, let me show you why." Then she did something with her hand and the monitor. The computer and monitor went into action, the voice on there was computerized and it talked about plastic bags and bottles that are thrown into many forms of water. It went on to say creeks, oceans, and lakes around the world. The computer voice said that each year about 46,000 pieces of plastic float on ocean waters where all types of fish eat this.

Dr. Brooks, taking off his glasses says, "Do you notice the electric cars on base? Well, to make plastic where you come from it takes a lot of petroleum to make all of the bottles, bags, and containers. Here we want to introduce a Base where we do not make or use plastic here. It is the future you're seeing right now. You saw this in your cars, computers, mobile phones, toys; everything you use in your day to day lives. Look, remember everything you threw away in Kansas?"

My mind could not forget it all and how we have to now adjust to something we have had all of our lives. I thought how are we going make it, our family. Then Sally spoke as if she was reading my mind. Colonel Mathews knew everything being said and he agreed to what I was saying but I knew he too, liked some of the old ways until this mission.

Sally goes on to say, "In the folder you have, we have left a lot of reading material about plastic and the effects it has had on many people. Please go home and read them and know the reasons for having no type of plastic on the Base."

Sally said, "I'm going to show the products we have here in your home so you will know them."

Then it went to another screen. Harold was trying to take everything in, there was a lot to absorb. They told us to take our time and read over our notes and look demo at our new home. Sally said, "You will see in your home and around the base a lot of bamboo, wood, glass, and stainless steel." Then the screen went through some of the items I would see here. Metal proof glasses, stainless steel straws and containers, fabric lunch bags, metal razors, it seemed like the product picture slides went fast.

More items flashed on the display area; shower curtains made out of cloth instead of plastic, Bamboo keyboards, and computer, a lot of items in bamboo style. It was a quick education on what our family would see at this undisclosed location. Then Both Sally and Dr. Brooks shook my hand firmly. I shook back and they walked toward the exit of the room and both vanished out the door.

Then the Colonel stood up and said, "That will be all for today. Please enjoy the rest of day and we will see in here bright and early in 48 hours from today. Is that okay 2nd LT Johnson?"

"That would be fine," as he saluted the Colonel and he saluted back.

The door opened automatically as he was walking out to his new family car. Looking at his surroundings he thought again, "this is not Kansas anymore".

As he was pulling into the double dome garage, the second door came down and he looked at his new car and said, "Wow that was awesome". His heartbeat opened the door and his wife greeted him.

"Hi Honey, how was your first day on base?

He said, "It was good, I meet three commanders today. That's all I can say for now."

He asked Hannah if there was any news on the kid's schools. She said she looked at some information on the schools.

"Located here, very advanced honey and they start next week. I'm trying to get all the information needed for their school,' said Margret.

"You're always the research person for our family honey. Remember you wanted to be a real estate agent?"

Hannah said, "Yes I still do. I wonder if they have any offices on this base," she winked at Harold.

Hannah went on to say, "I'm going to have my hands full here honey. My research talent will help us here, I'm sure."

 Harold heard some noise coming from another area of the dome home. He checked to see what was going on and it was Nolan and Zelda. They had virtual reality gear over the eyes and what seemed to be gloves. They were both laughing.

"What's going on back here?"

They said, "Dad, Zelda will show you," and she took her gear and handed it to her Dad to wear over his eyes, He went along with the idea and Harold put on the gloves. All of a sudden he could see his hands in the virtual set and then he saw an image of another person image next to him.

"Hey Dad, it's me. I'm here, both of us are in the virtual reality."

Harold started moving and said, "No way, look at that, how cool."

"Yes", said his son. "You can have up to ten people here all at one time Dad."

Harold said, You mean you can have your friends come over and they can stay home and be here at the same time?"

He said, "Yesss… Harold said to himself "no way". Then Nolan said, "Watch this Dad", and the next thing happened to both of them, they were on the top of the empire state building.

Harold said, "Wowww! There's no way, I see you here too!"

"You can take vacations from here."

"No way, well I would rather go in person."

"Yes, I know Dad. Touch the building."

Harold did and it felt like the building in his hands. He said, "Okay Dad, one more thing I want to show you. Watch this!" Nolan did something and they were in the space area, it said the 'Moon'.

Sitting there, Harold looked, he was on the moon and he saw in the distance his son waving him on and asking him to walk where he was. Harold went over and there on the moon was a basketball court, and his son said, "We can play basketball on the moon Dad, look." He started bouncing a basketball and he shot it up in the air as the moon was sitting on the horizon, the ball went swish…

Harold was amazed. He walked over, took the ball and he tried to make a shot and it missed. Then he was hooked. He said, "Give me the ball again son," and Harold started bouncing the ball on the moon and he did a turnaround jumper and the shot went in and he yelled out loud. His wife came from another room to see if everything was okay and Harold had the Virtual Goggles on yelling and jumping up and down, saying "I made the shoot whoop whoop."

Hannah looked at her husband as he was jumping and yelling. She said, "Hey, are you okay over there?"

He said, "Yes, I'm playing basketball on the moon Honey!" He took off the virtual headset and elbowed his son and walked out of the room in amazement.

Hannah said, "We have seen more than most about the future, honey."

Harold said, "Yes I know. Well, I'm going rest. I have to report back in 48 hours for my real first day."

Hannah said, "This is it the first day on a base unknown."

Chapter 31

Yautja could not control the life force current that was bringing her up to the center of the ship. The ocean water did not affect her from going up, it seemed like it took forever, it moved her slowly up the current.

The light spread over the bottom of the ocean as this strange mammoth ship from her planet brought Yautja closer to the opening.

While she was looking up, coming to the entrance of the opening she saw different shapes. The opening started to close as her feet were finally in. Then it shut and she could not see anything, not even her hand.

A small light came on from a distance and it looked like a hallway and she stood up to walk. Then the light went to bright colors and she could see the hallway a little better. She kept walking until she came to a chamber, like an elevator, that had a bar or handle in it. There she grabbed the bar and a voice said something in her language and she knew what it said. She grabbed the bar as tight as she could.

And that chamber did not go up like you would expect, it went sideways at 100 miles per hour. It was fast. The trip took five minutes. A door opened up as the travel chamber stopped. She was in a large space now it had controls everywhere.

She was walking around the space and it looked like time capsules of others from her race, three regular sizes and a one smaller one as if a pet came in it.

Fiwusho planet. Each had a title and a year they were from. All of them seemed like they were from a different year in time. she noticed the years each one were from had gaps. Even the pet was from a different time period in her race. She saw many pets from her planet before but this one was different.

Yautja wanted to walk around the ship more before she tapped a button to release this time capsule. She knew she had to find out more information. It was somewhere on this ship, still, at the bottom of the ocean the ship didn't move, it had stayed in the same place.

While walking and thinking, she jumped back on the chamber, gripped her hands on the bar and it was going again, fast around the ship. This time it went left sideways traveling at top speeds. It stopped, then it moved down a little bit to a room. When it opened the room looked like diamond glass, sparkling from top to bottom on the side. She walked to the middle the room…then the room went pitch black and there were lines everywhere. It looked maps and coordinates and times in her native language. Like a planetarium with maps, she thought, how amazing this is. The room gave yearly dates and locations. She wondered if this room controlled how the ship flies.

She yelled out locations in the air to see if the room would change. She knew of other planets and places, she yelled Suakhapie the room pulled up the locations and maps. Then she said Ooynt and again the locations came up over her head.

The last thing she yelled out was Earth and the picture went to a panoramic view at the bottom of the ocean and her current location.

Chapter 32

Reporter Marc Dazet was is a different place in his thoughts. He had this blueprint of a ship and he wanted to know more about the lady in Florida and the cruise ship. In his wallet, he had a number that was connected to the future. Brent's uncle, Dr. Eugene Brooks had given it to him. He thought maybe he should call him, he could tell him more about what's going to happen. He decided he would call and he told Sundara he was going to take a walk and he would be right back.

Riding down to the ocean front, Marc went seeking more about the future. He parked his car at the public entrance to walk on the beach. It was about 3 pm in the afternoon, he takes the number out of his wallet to call the Doctor. He remembered what he told him, he said dial the year and the current day and it would go through to him…he thought about it, it was 2017 and the day and date is Nov. 29th, so he dialed the number 2017 1129 and he put the phone to his ear to hear and it rang three times.

Then the voice came on the phone. It said, "Hello Marc, Hello." The sounds in the background were like something he never heard in his life.

"Hello Dr. Brooks, it's me, Marc. I wanted to talk with you." Marc was walking on the sand close to the water but not in the water. Walking and talking he said, "Hello Dr. Brooks..."

"Hi there, Marc. Look, wait one second while I go to someplace quieter." Marc tried to make out what that sound was, but he couldn't place it to save his life. Then it went quiet and the Dr. went on to speak. "How are you after our meeting in Hampton? A lot has happened since then. there building a bike trail for the Hampton roads area?"

"And beyond, it should cover a few states... and I have more to tell you." It sounded like he was getting his notes out, he said, "Look, are you by yourself ?"

Marc answered yes so Dr. Brooks continued, "Look you're going think I'm weird but you're supposed to do something. You're supposed to build a ship."

Marc almost dropped the phone. "Really?"

"Yes really," he said. "Do you have some type of blueprints there.

Marc said under his breath, "how did he know I have blueprints. "Yes, I have blueprints here Doctor."

He said, "I'm going help you with this ship, you will need my help for the parts because the parts are not from your time, they're from many time periods and I have to find them for you."

Marc couldn't talk for the next five minutes. "You will have help from me and others…You have to build a spaceship Marc and this ship will fly in the air but it's mostly used for under the water."

"Really?" he said, rubbing his forehead, trying to absorb what he has been told.

 "Yes," replied Dr. Brooks.

Then the sound got louder. Marc wanted to ask who, what, where, and how are we going to build a spaceship? "It's okay, I will explain later. I have to run now," said the good doctor.

The sound was even louder, from which time zone he did not know. Marc said, "Okay will talk soon again."

"Hold on to the blueprints okay, don't lose them and stay in touch with my nephew."

"Okay," said Marc and he heard the other end hang up and click.

Standing there, as the ocean waters where crashing on the shore, Marc could not believe what he just heard. It looked like he went into a sprint walk, then he ran to his jeep, jumped in and drove back home. He just wanted to see his family and give them a hug.

He was at home and he had to tell his wife about the blueprints without telling her about Dr. Eugene Brooks. "How am I going explain to my wife about this information," he thought. "I am clueless!

****

Brent was happy he was home with the family and he thought about the new currency with the Free State Project and winning the lottery in New Hampshire. He thought about his twins and wife Margret and his year at Lowes and he was looking at the relic in his hand from New Jersey.

He was thinking about what happened when that light went on. He wanted to research what he had in his hand, maybe if he looked it up online there might be some clue.

He used his Google to research – *have other people found relics on the ground?* His answer was: The Relics are important aspects of some forms of many religions, means to leave behind." Brent thought, "did something get left behind and became retrieved back again when the light from the stone was there?…It also said: a relic is also the term for something that has survived the passage of time. Then Brent wondered "if this is a key or something, is there such a thing as a Relic Key?" , and there it was, right there on the computer screen, there are relic keys that exist in history!

He wondered again "if when the two pieces came together, did it open a door for something to happen?" At that moment Jerry and Jarvis came into his office, they're asking how he was doing and are there any more road trips planned ahead.

Brent said, "No, we're going stay around Seabrook for a while ... Help out locally around here. You have school now, so the next time you have free time will be Christmas, yes?" Both the twins agreed. They're talking about gifts and this would be the first Christmas where everyone can buy gifts for each other.

"Yes," Brent said it will be the first one. "So what do you want for Christmas"? he asked the boys.

They said they wanted a translator person who would tell us stories in like in New Jersey, about the Lenni Lenape Tribes.

"I can arrange this to happen" and both the twins said, "Dad, how about building a water park here in Seabrook with a big wave pool, all kinds of rides? Many people would come here."

Brent said, "Look, it's cold in the winter time here, it would be closed."

Then they suggested an indoor and outdoor water park together. He liked the idea and he said he would think about it.

The twins walked out of the room and Brent went to talk with Margret. She was happy to see everyone home at the same time for a change.

"It's nice to see everyone home."

Brent said, "Yes, it is, isn't it?" He told her he was doing research about relics.

Margret told him she knew a little about them from teaching history.

Brent said, "I looked the information up on the computer to find out more about it. I think it's a key of some sort and when the light came from it, it unlocked something somewhere. I don't know where but something must have happened."

Nelson, the Brooks' bodyguard watched the home and the family closely. He checked all the rooms walking around the home to make sure everyone was safe. He was walking outside near the gate and he happened to see a black and purple pickup truck just parked there. He wondered why they were parked there by the gate.

He held up both hands in the air to send a single to them what do they want? And the truck turned on its engine and drove away…He opened the security gate and walked to inspect the area. Maybe they left something behind that would let him know who they were and there was a card on the ground. It said Earth Surveillance Department and it had a number on it. He picked it up and put it in his pocket.

Brent sent a text to Marc, it said "Hey Marc, how are you doing?"

Marc texted back, "I'm doing okay. How about your family?"

"Our family is finally back home and resting for a change locally."

Marc asked him, "Have you seen that channel on your Satellite lately?"

Brent said, "Nope, I tried to and there's nothing there. The only thing weird now in this life is the Relic Key I was given."

Marc said, "Key? What type of key?"

Brent said, "I have no clue what type of relic key I have, I can send you a picture of the key and maybe you can find out something."

Marc said, "Of course." They ended their texting and Marc waited for the picture to come over.

It didn't take a half a second and snap, snap, he texted Marc the picture of the key. Marc was looking at it, turning his camera upside down to stare at the picture. He wondered the same as Brent, what is this key, what does it open or release? He closed his phone and his thoughts drifted on building a spaceship that flies and goes underwater. Where can we build this ship and why are we building it, is it for us to be in?

****

Harold and Hannah Johnson rested for the night. They had some time before the first day of his training. In their living room, they decided to find the TV in their new dome home and wanted to see what type of channels are here. Hannah asked, "Where is the TV, I don't see any around?"

Then Hannah saw a button that said TV on her chair. She pushed it and then a Hisense TV seemed like it floated in air. We all leaned back in our chairs, then it turned on and there was a voice, "Please pick a topic."

Hannah said, "short movies". And before you know it there was something like 35 channels that all catered to short films. We smiled at each other.

"Okay, your turn, pick a topic, Harold." I said "sports" then, bam, 30 channels came up with all the sports broadcasts they had then from everywhere. They even had a cricket channel. I wanted to see if the channel 'Go Flavor Go' would be broadcast on this TV and yelled out Go Flavor Go and it did. The channel came up and I smiled, it's here even at this Space base.

Hannah finally choose a word, it was "cooking" and we watched a few of the cooking channels on the futuristic TV. We knew we were here for a reason, for ourselves and for our country. You could not ask for more when it's going to be an adventure and they're going to make it tough on me during training. The leadership must know something or this SpaceMarine base would not be here…

****

Marc called Amelia and told her he would stick around and not go to Florida. "I need to stay home in Virginia for a change. If you ever have a huge story again, promise me you would let me travel to write it."

Amelia said, "I don't think you can outdo the New Hampshire Lottery winning story."

Marc said, "You never know, you have to give me your word today, you'll let me go."

Amelia said, "I will, I promise." … Marc hung up the phone, sat there a minute to think what a month this is, in November there's Thanksgiving, the start of the Christmas holidays and the closing of a New Year around the corner. And I'm married to my wonderful wife Sundara and I have a great daughter …

He glanced over to the envelope with the blueprints and took them out to read them. He knew this going to be the biggest project in his life. Laura was on the phone talking to her friends and Sundara was starting again at the picture on the wall of the stars and her home of Ooynt in the Andromeda Galaxy.

She looked at Marc and said, One day you will come home with me to visit my homeland and you can meet members of my family."

Marc said that "It would be nice to see where you were born."

She goes on to say, "I have a lot Ooyantians I want you to meet"

Marc answered, "I want to meet them too Aradnus and for them to meet our daughter Laura." He thought to himself maybe we are building this spacecraft to visit the Andromeda Galaxy. I wish I could see into the future to know.

Chapter 33

The ocean floor was calm as Yautja went back to the room where the time capsule was located. She thought this mission was different from other missions she was assigned where she helped others around the globe. This time an inward mission. She went to each one to try to read their thoughts and there were none. She knew it was time to release them, I must find something on this ship that unchains these capsules. She was trying all the buttons and nothing happened. She kept trying, saying words, still nothing …

There must be a key or something to unlock these so she looked over the ship and there it was, a spot near the capsule that was missing. She thought there had to be something there…it fits in that space. Who has this key she wondered… Ummm, pacing the floor she decides to go back to the map room and she yells out at the room "key" in her language and it showed a picture of the Relic Key for the time capsule, the size and what it looked like. And she thought, who has this key. I need it and she asked the map where the key was and it only gave a map of Earth, that was it. That was the only clue she had, it was on earth, this key.

"How can I find this key?" She asked…

****

Brent took the relic and placed it in a safe place. He even hid it from his family. Nelson wanted to make sure Brent knew what happened outside of their gated home, he gave him the card he found on the road and told him it was kind of strange that he saw someone there...and they dropped a card.

He took the card, went to a small room where his TV was located and started flipping through the channels to see if he could see that certain channel and there it was the same channel he saw a month ago and this time it looked like it was underwater. He tried to see if he could make anything out but he could only see a shadow of a huge object in the ocean water. What is this he thought...he still couldn't see what it was. Then he saw it, a ship not from here and it looked like it didn't move at all, frozen in the water…

****

Yautja looked as something was beaming and it said the number 1 in her language and the words 'Seabrook, New Hampshire' and she tapped a button and it went away.

Then Brent's channel vanished from his TV set. He fumbled over his chair in sheer panic, dropped the remote control and ran to another room. Margret asked him what's wrong.

"You look pale, you okay honey?"

He said, "I'm fine …Wow, what a day he What a day…

Acknowledgments

First I would like to thank my parents for raising me. James and Edna J. aka M+D

And Shirley Wiggerman (Author) for pushing me for a year to write an outline, and helping with ideas for the storyline.

Nanowrimo 2016 in November Great writing company and concept.

Cindy Calzone(Editor) Vikiana (Book Cover) Jesi Jayy (Words)

And everyone in Hampton, Virginia with their insights and support 360. For Dialogue Prompt

Thanks to God

@Copyright Dialogue Prompt

BFJ